Wagstaffe the Wind-up Boy

"I've never heard anything like it," he stormed at Dr Dhondy. "You're not a surgeon, you're a fruitcake. I only got run down by a truck. Why couldn't I be stitched up like anybody else? Why the key?"

"You have a key, Wagstaffe," the doctor replied quietly, "because you have a spring. How else could we wind you up?"

For many minutes Wagstaffe said not a word. Then he asked for a big mirror. Wagstaffe turned round.

"Oh crikey," he said. "Is it truly me?"

Wagstaffe
The Wind-up Boy

Jan Needle

Wagstaffe
The Wind-up Boy

Illustrated by
Roy Bentley

LIONS

First published in Great Britain
by André Deutsch Ltd in 1987
First published in Lions in 1989

Lions is an imprint of the Children's Division,
part of the Collins Publishing Group,
8 Grafton Street, London W1X 3LA

Copyright © 1987 by Jan Needle
Illustrations copyright © 1987 by Roy Bentley

Printed and bound in Great Britain by
William Collins Sons & Co. Ltd, Glasgow

For Hughie
Who gave me the idea in the first place,
and who will recognise all sorts of things

Chapter One

A Stroke of Luck

This is the story of a boy called Wagstaffe. He was a very ordinary boy in many ways, but he had one big problem — his mum and dad. From that big problem all the smaller problems of his life had come. There were millions of them.

Take his name, for instance. Wagstaffe was not his last name – like Smith, or Jones, or Sayeed, say – it was his first, like John, or Simon, or Mohammed. His full name was Wagstaffe Winstanley Watkins Williams. And he hated it.

His mum and dad, of course, had ordinary, proper names. His mother was called Wilhelmina (Willie for short) and his father was called Englebert. Wagstaffe could remember how hard they had argued over what to call him. The argument had gone on for so long, in fact, that he was eight before he had been christened. It took four vicars to get him into the font.

What sort of mum and dad was it that would call their only child Wagstaffe? Well, they were something like this:

First, Mr Englebert Simpkins Watkins Williams. At the time this tale starts, he was twenty-nine years old. He had trained to be a world-class snooker player, but he was colour-blind, so he became a teacher instead. He taught children.

Second, Willie (Mrs) Winstanley Watkins Williams. She was twenty-four, and had very strong views about babies. She did not like them. This meant that for the first six years

of his life, Wagstaffe never saw his mother, except when she changed him. Once she changed him for a new sideboard, but the police made her take him back.

Wagstaffe's early days were not happy. In fact, before you go on reading this book, you'd better get a handkerchief, or at least roll your sleeve down to sniff into. It is very sad.

Except for this: One morning, Wagstaffe came down to breakfast to find no cornflakes, no milk, no toast and no tea.

No mum and dad either. They'd left a note for him propped up on his money-box, which they'd emptied with a knife. It said:

Dear Wagstaffe,

You're so horrible that we've run away together for a better life. You will never, ever, see us again.

Your loving parents,

Mr and Mrs Williams

PS. Don't forget to clean the lavatory. It's Tuesday.

Chapter Two

April Fool?

Wagstaffe sat at the kitchen table and wondered whether to laugh or cry. At first he thought he'd have a good laugh. Until a dreadful thought struck him.

Maybe they were joking!

It was a sunny morning, and it was April. Which made Wagstaffe very suspicious. What if it was April the First? What if this was just a cruel trick? Another cruel trick? He went all cold inside.

Ever since he had been a very little lad, Wagstaffe's mother and father had taken their pleasure by playing tricks on him. He remembered some of them well.

There was the time they had taken him on holiday to Southsea, which is the posh part of a southern town called Portsmouth. It has a beach, all pebbles and lumps of oil from the tankers, and the summer they visited it, it had things called pedaloes. To Wagstaffe, his shorts and knobbly knees still grimy with northern muck, the pedaloes looked good.

"Go up and ask the man," his mum had said. "They give free goes to kids from the North of England."

So Wagstaffe had.

"Excuse me, Mister," he had said. "I come from Oldham, in Lancashire. Can I have my free ride?"

The man had said something very rude. Much too rude to put in a book for children. Wagstaffe had done it.

Willie (Mrs Watkins) and Englebert had laughed their socks off.

"You daft ha'porth," said Willie. "That was a joke. It's fifty pee a go!"

Later on the same holiday, they had played an even crueller trick, though. Wagstaffe's father had paid for him to have a pedalo, and had offered him five pounds if he could take it round the Isle of Wight. You could see the Isle of Wight across the water.

"It looks a long way," said Wagstaffe. "Are these things safe?"

"Safe?" shouted his dad. "Listen, lad, folk have sailed round the world in those things."

A pedalo, for those of you who don't know, is a pair of floating tubes with a tin armchair between them. You sit in it and whirl your legs round, so that the paddles push you along, very slowly, and soak you to the skin.

"Round the world?" asked Wagstaffe.

"Round the world," said Dad. "One feller did it twice. Non-stop."

Wagstaff was not stupid. He knew this was not true. But five pounds was three years' pocket money.

"All right," he said. "If I can have an ice cream first."

His mother smacked him.

"Don't you be so greedy, Wagstaffe. What will people think?"

Wagstaffe, snivelling, climbed into the pedalo and set off. He was rescued two days later by the Bembridge lifeboat. His mum and dad had already gone home to Oldham.

So before he started laughing, he had to be sure.

Wagstaffe pretended he was a secret service man.

"I'll search the house," he said.

Chapter Three

The Search

The house that Wagstaffe had been born in, and brought up in, did not take much searching. There were not many rooms.

He started with the kitchen, because he was in it. Because he knew how sneaky his mum and dad could be, he looked everywhere.

They weren't in the oven, they weren't in the fridge, and they weren't in the larder. Nor was anything else. They'd taken every scrap of food in the house.

Wagstaffe went into the living room. It was behind the kitchen, and usually contained the TV – which was black and white, for his father's eyes – and the quarter-size billiard table he wasn't allowed to play on.

"You're not colour-blind," his father always said. "You might beat me. That's not fair."

Today, it still contained the TV – which was blurred and broken, as well as black and white – but no billiard table. Also, no ordinary table, no chairs, and no magazine rack. No carpet, either.

Wagstaffe went into the downstairs lavatory. It was all brown and smelly. Tuesday. His day to clean it. But no mum and dad. No lavatory paper either. He went upstairs.

There were only two bedrooms in the house, and Wagstaffe had never been in his mum and dad's. But when he opened the door, he guessed something had been taken out of it. It was completely bare, without even a stain to make the wallpaper look homely.

"I bet they had a bed," he said. "And Mum would have had a wardrobe to put her clothes in, and a dressing table. I think they're really gone."

And in his own room, there was everything just as he'd left it. The broken trainset, the bucket under the hole in the roof, the pile of coats on the floor where he slept.

Wagstaffe giggled.

"I think they've really gone," he said again. "I really do think they've gone. Yippee."

Then the front door bell rang.

Chapter Four

A Few Fibs

As it happened, Wagstaffe was standing in front of the piece of mirror glued to his bedroom wall when the bell went. He was about to set off to open the door when he saw himself.

"Cripes," he thought. "I can't go down there, looking like this."

Wagstaffe was a scruffy boy, no one would tell you different. He was dead skinny, all bumps and knobs and

joints, and he looked as if he'd slept in his clothes and not washed for a week.

The main reason for this was that he had slept in his clothes and not washed for a week. To be nearer the truth, he had slept in his clothes for a week, and not washed for a fortnight. Or to be completely honest, he had slept in his clothes for a fortnight, and not washed for a month.

"They don't like it," he told himself. "Grown ups just don't like it. If it's someone from the council, or a copper, they'll take me away. What with the furniture having gone, an' all."

It had not occurred to Wagstaffe until then to wonder how and when the furniture had gone. His mum and dad must have had a wagon call in the night. Silly of them not to wake him. He could have helped them load it.

The bell was being rung again, hard. Wagstaffe popped into his mum and dad's bedroom and peeked out of the window. Oh 'ell. It was the milkman. He'd be wanting cash.

But he also had milk.

And yoghurt.

And eggs.

And cream.

And tins of peaches.

Wagstaffe ran downstairs.

"Now then," said the milkman. "Is your mother in? She owes me four pound eighty."

"She's not," said Wagstaffe. "She's been called off to me Auntie Emily's, who's sick. And me dad's gone too. And they said they'll pay you when they're back, and can I have two pints every day till then, please?"

He smiled. The milkman was a very oldish, farmery sort of chap, who seemed to enjoy his work.

"I shouldn't really," he said. "But all right, then!"

Wagstaffe pushed his luck.

"And six yoghurts and a dozen eggs and a pint of cream and a tin of peaches, please," he added.

Mr Huddersfield (the milkman) grinned.

"Every day?" he said. "You're a greedy beggar, Wagstaffe. Why aren't you at school? It's nearly nine o'clock."

"Holiday today."

"You're a liar, too. In fact, you're just like I was when I were a lad. When did you last have a wash?"

Wagstaffe scratched his head. Little dead bits came out of it.

"February, I think. Why?"

The milkman laughed.

"If I was your dad I wouldn't put up with it. Or your mother, either. And him a teacher, too."

Wagstaffe nodded.

"I'm a great bother to them, Mr Huddersfield. They're always telling me. I can't do sums, neither."

The two of them went to the milk float. Mr Huddersfield helped Wagstaffe carry the stuff back into the kitchen.

"If you keep knocking off school you'll never learn your sums," he said. "Can you read and write?"

"Oh aye," said Wagstaffe. "Enough to get by."

The milkman snorted.

"Enough to get by! What about when you grow up?"

"I'll watch TV."

They shook hands on it.

19

Chapter Five

Early Days

It wasn't all his parents' fault, you see. Because although he's the hero of this book, Wagstaffe isn't everybody's cup of tea. He's not the sort of boy your Auntie Mabel would approve of (if you had one). In fact, in many ways, he is a Manky Little Rat.

Wagstaffe went and sat down at the kitchen table for his breakfast. As his mum and dad had taken all the crocks with them, plus all the knives and forks and spoons, he drank a pint of milk, washed down with a pint of cream. He couldn't open the peaches – no tin opener – and he didn't really like yoghurt, because his mother said it was good for him.

The dozen eggs he decided to save for throwing at policemen.

Then he thought. Why do they hate me? Why have they made my life so miserable? Why have they run away?

Wagstaffe was an honest boy (except that he told lies all the time) and he was quite willing to admit that his mum and dad were right about one thing: he was horrible to them. He tried to make a list of some of the Horrible Things he'd done.

One. When he was a baby, he'd always waited until his nappy had been taken off *before* he had a poo. Once he'd done it when the doctor was holding him up to the light. Right on to his bald head.

Two. Even when he'd been *really* tired he'd always spoiled their favourite TV programmes by pretending to wake up and starting to scream. He said he was afraid of the nasty monsters in his dreams.

Three. He wouldn't eat his food, sometimes for days and days and days. This is why he was so skinny. But when guests were coming, he always ate like a pig, then threw up all over them if possible.

Four. He was *very* good at making mysterious and vile smells when there were strangers in the house. When he was too small to be bashed for it, he'd always pointed at the visitors and said: "You've let off, haven't you?"

Five. He learned how to hold his breath until he turned grey. He used to do this at the front gate when a police-man was coming, then lie down and go stiff on the pavement. He was often taken to hospital, where he told the doctors his mum and dad ill-treated him.

There were many more Horrible Things, but Wagstaffe could not remember them for the moment. He felt quite sad. He wouldn't have done them if he'd had a Good Father and a Good Mother.

He was a very unlucky boy.

Chapter Six

What Makes a
Good Father?

Ever since he'd been a little brat, Wagstaffe had wanted
a Good Father.

He'd wanted to be taught how to shoot, how to build
model planes, how to drive a railway engine, and how to
swim the Channel.

He had also wanted to have a very large dog called
Slobberchops, four white rats called Eenie, Meenie, Miney
and Mo, a python, a racehorse and a stick insect.

He had wanted to live on ice cream and sweets, never to
clean his teeth, not to wear underpants or pyjamas, and to
have a racing bike with eleven gears.

For his holidays he had wanted to go canal boating, sailing
and swimming, either in North Wales or the Canary
Islands, whichever was nearer.

He got a stub of pencil from his jeans pocket and made
marks on the table top. He thought about all these things
in turn, and wrote:

No shooting – his father thought guns were noisy.

No planes – too much trouble.

No engine driving – you got more money as a teacher.

No Channel swimming – it wasn't worth it because
French food was smelly.

Pets. No pets.

Food. Sweets on Saturday if he was good. He was not
good – so no sweets. Ice cream the same.

Teeth cleaning. He had to do it, although he always cheated and he always spat on the kitchen floor to annoy his mum.

Underpants and pyjamas. He had to wear underpants but he got his own back by never changing them. Since he gave his pyjamas to the rag and bone man one day he'd been all right there. He slept in his day clothes, but he sometimes took his trainers off to give the sheets a treat.

Wagstaffe wondered what made a good father. One you could climb on, like a tree. One you could fight with. One who gave you crisps and Coke and sweets and money. One who took you to North Wales or the Canary Islands, or canal boating or sailing. One who didn't play cruel tricks or call you names. One who let you taste his beer and didn't make you learn to read and write and do sums.

Mr Englebert Simpkins Watkins Williams was none of these things. He was a sensible, boring person who wore a suit and never let you play with him. He said that eating carrots made you see in the dark, and watching TV made you blind.

He was a liar.

Chapter Seven

Sticks and Stones

Wagstaffe's mum was even more dreadful than his dad.

She'd come from a Very Good Home, where she'd been Brought Up Proper. The Worst Mistake She'd Ever Made had been marrying Wagstaffe's father. The Second Worst Mistake had been having Wagstaffe.

"You should have been drowned at birth," she told him once. "What a pity you're not a puppy."

Wagstaffe thought it was a pity too. If she'd tried to drown him he could have bitten her. Or at least peed on her leg. He peed on her leg anyway.

While Mr Englebert Simpkins Watkins Williams went off to bore children for a living, Mrs Wilhelmina Winstanley Watkins Williams stayed at home and bored Wagstaffe. She tried to turn him into a Proper Little Boy.

First it was How to Wash. Then it was How to Dress. Then it was How to Behave. Then it was How to Eat Without Making a Noise, then it was How to Talk to People Nicely. Then it was What To Do To Get On Well At School.

Wagstaffe, his mind on railway engines and pythons, ignored all this nonsense, and picked his nose and ate the soft and tasty contents of each nostril. He liked it best when a sticky green bit glued itself to a tooth and had to be picked off with a finger nail.

First his mother, then his dad, began to call him names.

Chapter Eight

May Break My Bones

The first name they called Wagstaffe was the unfairest of the lot. They called him Smelly Bum.

The reason it was unfair was not because it was a lie, because it wasn't. His bum did smell. Wagstaffe rather liked it, and used to go under the covers to be with it at night. But other people found it nasty.

The reason this was unfair, was because Wagstaffe was not allowed to use the bathroom, so it was pretty obvious his bum was going to smell. Everything about him smelled.

The reason he was not allowed to use the bathroom was simple. His mum had been Brought Up Proper. Wagstaffe was dirty, and the bathroom was clean. If Wagstaffe used the bathroom, he would become clean (maybe) and the bathroom would get dirty. His mum knew which she wanted most: A Clean Bathroom.

The reason Wagstaffe was dirty in the first place was even simpler. As he never let fly as a baby until his nappy had been taken off, his mum spent more time cleaning herself and the sofa than she did cleaning him. By the time she got round to it, he was too dirty to be taken into the bathroom.

The reason Wagstaffe had forgotten to look in the bathroom when he was searching the house in Chapter Three was because he had forgotten there was one. But I'll tell you now – they weren't in there. They'd gone.

Have you noticed something about this chapter? All but

29

seven of the paragraphs start with the word The, and all but nine with the phrase The Reason. This means that it is LITERATURE. Ask your teacher. Now let's have some more rude names.

Chapter Nine

But Names Will Never Hurt Me

As Wagstaffe grew older, the names changed. They went from Smelly Bum to Snotbubble, from Snotbubble to Dribblegobble, from Dribblegobble to Weed, from Weed to Scabbyhead, from Scabbyhead to Ugly, from Ugly to Boring, from Boring to Stupid, and from Stupid to Useless.

When they wanted to be nasty, they called him by real names, which they said they would christen him with if he wasn't careful.

Like Algy, and Basil, and Cedric, and Desmond, and Egbert, and Fingal, and Georgie, and Herbert, and Ignatius, and Jimbob, and Kim, and Leofric, and Maurice, and Neil, and 'Orace, and Piers, and Quilch, and Rupert, and Sacha, and Theo, and Udo, and Vera, and Wagstaffe, and Xavier, and Yusuf, and Zorba.

Wagstaffe, who was getting quite clever by this time, copied all the horrible names down and left the list lying about to be found. At the bottom of it he wrote: "I quite like them all, really. Except Wagstaffe. I *hate* Wagstaffe." So now you know how he got his name.

Although he fought hard and long to stay out of the font, and filled the quiet church of Saint Bumpkin with appalling language while he kicked and spat at the four unhappy vicars, Wagstaffe ended up not minding his name all that much at all. He was too busy thinking up good ones to call his mum and dad. The day came at last to try them out.

First, father. One day his father said to him: "How are you this morning, disgusting little blob of sicked up maggot's food?"

Wagstaffe replied: "Not bad thank you, Fatguts Stinkbreath. And yourself?"

To Wagstaffe, it seemed a not bad thing to say. His father was fat. He could hide a cream cake in his belly button. And his breath smelled like long dead cheese.

His father hit him.

Next, mother. One day his mother said to him: "Don't

hold your fork like that, Halfwit, you'll go deaf and your hair will drop out."

"Speak up, Thunderthighs," he said. "I can't hear a word you're saying."

His mother burst into tears.

Wagstaffe remembered all this sitting at the breakfast table, and it made him hope even harder that it was not April the First and all some horrid joke. He didn't think he could bear it if they came back again.

There was a strange plopping noise at the front door and the newspaper fell onto the mat. Wagstaffe checked the date. It was April the Third.

So that was all right.

But where had they gone? And would they come back once Mr Englebert Williams had finished boring his pupils for the day?

Perhaps Wagstaffe should run away...

Chapter Ten

Mayhem

Wagstaffe Winstanley Watkins Williams knew all about running away. He'd seen the films, and watched the TV serials, and even glanced at some of the books. To him, it all seemed a bit too much like hard work.

What's more, there were certain things you needed, if you were going to do it right. You needed a river to float your raft on, and an island to hide on, and lots of food and money to live on, and a friend or two to rely on. Some stories had a sensible girl as well, but Wagstaffe didn't fancy that. All the girls he knew liked to wash.

What he would do, he decided, was make some checks. First of all he'd ring the school where his father bored for a living. Luckily, his mother and father had left the phone, so that was easy.

"Hello," he told the headmaster. "Is Mr Englebert Williams there? This is his father speaking."

It occurred to Wagstaffe that the headmaster would have to be mental to believe that, and so it proved.

"Oh, hello, sir," said the head. "No, I'm afraid Mr Williams has left. He's gone to join a circus, I believe. I'm surprised he didn't tell you."

"Gosh, how naughty of him," said Wagstaffe, now changing his voice to that of a ninety-three year-old father. "I shall have to spank his bottie."

"Yes, indeed," said the headmaster. "It's no more than

he deserves. Give him one from me."

They shared a laugh, and Wagstaffe put the phone down.

"A circus, eh? In his condition! It's no wonder they raided my money box."

Next he went around all the neighbours, to see if they'd seen or heard anything.

But all the neighbours, in all the posh, quiet houses with mowed lawns and high hedges, saw him coming up their garden paths, and hid. Mr Fatty Dickin, who was very fond of *nice* children, set the dog on him. Wagstaffe threw a tin of peaches at it.

Back at home he made his mind up. If they'd really gone, there was no need to run away. He'd live in the house, and get food off the milkman, and never, *ever*, clean the lavatory again, not even on a Tuesday. He'd do no work at all, and lead a happy and contented life.

Tired by these thoughts, he decided to start with a nice day off. He collected his catapult and the dozen eggs, picked his piece of chewing gum off the back of the fridge and popped it into his mouth, and went out to enjoy himself.

It was time he spread some mayhem around the town.

Chapter Eleven

The Accident

If you're reading this in class, which I very much doubt, you'd better tell the teacher to leave the room now.

If you're reading this in bed, call your mother or father, or the doctor or the vet. You'll need a bucket and a box of tissues at least. Because here, Wagstaffe's tale turns nasty.

Simple really. After letting off eleven stink bombs in the library, throwing two eggs at a policeman on point duty, and making disgusting noises through the letterbox of an extremely expensive café where old ladies in furs were drinking morning coffee – Wagstaffe got bored. He couldn't think of any more mayhem to do. So he decided to play on the motorway.

You don't need me or a plumber to tell you how silly that was, do you? Later on, if he lives, Wagstaffe will tell you himself. But for now, close your eyes if you get sick easily, and read on.

Here is the mighty M62, stretching from Hull to Liverpool. Here is Tandle Hill, near Oldham. Here is Wagstaffe, running down the hill, across the streams, over the farm tracks. Here he is climbing over the fence, and jumping on to the hard shoulder. Half a mile away, here comes a lorry.

It is a nice lorry, a Mercedes 16-32, with eighteen tons of fishmeal on its trailer. It is doing exactly sixty miles per hour, which means that in half a minute it will reach the

spot where Wagstaffe is standing. And what is Wagstaffe
doing?

Believe it or not, he is fitting an egg into his catapult. He
is pulling back the rubber. He is aiming at the windscreen
of the lorry. And he is letting go.

Wheeeee, goes the egg, right onto the windscreen.

Then: Splatt!

Inside the cab, the lorry driver cannot see much. Except
Wagstaffe, standing there like an idiot, laughing fit to bust.

Fishmeal is nasty stuff, and the driver is not happy. He
turns the wheel with a grunt, then turns it back again.

Wheeeee, goes the trailer, right on to the hard shoulder.

Then: Splatt!

Wagstaffe, much to his surprise, is flattened right across
the middle by the big double-tyred wheel. His breakfast

pops out of his mouth and his stomach pops out of his trouser legs. There is blood and guts all over the place.

The driver looks into his nearside mirror and watches Wagstaffe twitching on the hard shoulder. He seems to be waving. The driver smiles.

"He'll not do that again in a hurry," he says.

He switches on the washers to clean the egg off the windscreen.

Wagstaffe, blowing pretty pink bubbles with his lips and nostrils, says:

"That's not fair. You're bigger than me."

Chapter Twelve

The Blood Wagon

First aid, like most things, comes in various shapes and sizes. Scratch your knuckle, and someone might kiss it better. Cut your finger, and you'll maybe get a plaster. Break an arm, and you'll get a sling, break a leg, and you'll get a cast that your friends will write their names on.

Some people think big. They get hurt so badly that men with stretchers come. Some need ambulances, or in out-of-the-way places, rescue helicopters that chop-chop-chop them off to hospital. Sometimes fire brigades are radioed, and big red engines come screaming along with their sirens blaring and their bells ringing merry hell. Sometimes the army gets called out, and foreign governments send aid.

None of this happened to Wagstaffe, although many motorists stopped to look at him, and one or two poked him with their toe-caps or their jack handles. Because Wagstaffe, they could see, was dead. *Very* dead.

"He's flatter than a duck's foot," said Hughie N'Dell, who knows all about duck's feet. "He'll never play the E flat bass again."

"He was too little anyway," said another passer-by. "He's more a cornet size, that one. Although he might just have managed a flugel, given exercise."

This was Oldham, see, where everyone knows about brass bands. Someone from St Helen's, where they know about anoraks, said: "Shouldn't we cover him up? He might get cold."

Everybody laughed.

"He'll get colder yet," they said, with typical warm-hearted northern humour. "Unless he goes straight to hell and stokes the boilers!"

Then they all got bored, and drove away. Someone remembered to dial 999.

"Police, fire brigade or ambulance?"

"Put me through to the corporation please, Miss. I want to speak to the fellers that drive the muckcarts."

It was Tuesday, right? Dustbin day in the Tandle Hill area. In another hour the muckcart trundled up to

Wagstaffe's body on the hard shoulder. Two men got out with shovels.

"Eh up, Fred," said Charlie. "Hast got a black plastic bag?"

"Eh, but this is a bad do," said Fred. "We ought to get overtime for this. Messy little beggar."

That was true. Wagstaffe had dribbled bits across a wide area by now, especially where people had trodden on his ends. He was like a gingerbread man spread with strawberry jam. Only his head and feet were normal, except that his toes were swollen and his eyes had bulged like plums.

"We won't though, will we?" said Charlie. "Nobody gives *that* much for us."

And he clicked his fingers, before sliding the broad end of his shovel under the soggy mess that was our gallant hero.

"Do you mind?" said Wagstaffe. "That hurts."

The shovel had touched a nerve. For five words only, Wagstaffe could speak.

Charlie and Fred looked at each other across the corpse. They turned white. Fred dropped the black plastic bag, and Charlie dropped the shovel. They both dropped to the ground in a dead faint.

It was *then* that someone called an ambulance.

Chapter Thirteen

The Hospital

So far in this story, Wagstaffe hasn't had a lot of luck. He's had tricks played on him, he's been called names, he's been squashed flat by a lorry. But suddenly, lying there on the hard shoulder of the M62 with two spark out dustmen, things began to go right for him.

It happened like this.

The ambulance driver, a nasty, skinny man called Aubrey, decided that Wagstaffe was beyond repair. He wasn't going to bother taking him to hospital, because it was a waste of time and money. He thought of chucking him in the Rochdale Canal, along with all the other rubbish.

Then he remembered. The duty surgeon at the hospital today was Dr Dhondy.

Aubrey did not like Dr Dhondy. In fact he hated her. He thought it would be a right good laugh to deliver Wagstaffe, make her sweat for hours trying to save him, then tell everyone what a crummy doctor she was when Wagstaffe was taken away and buried.

He chucked two buckets of water over Fred and Charlie to bring them round, then picked Wagstaffe up by one ear and tossed him into the ambulance.

"Be careful!" yelled Charlie. "That lad could live!"

"Poop," said Aubrey. He drove happily away, with his blue light flashing.

At casualty, the porters laughed.

"Wrong door, Aubrey," they said, when they saw what was left of Wagstaff. "Dead 'uns go round the back."

At the counter, the nurse in charge almost had a fit.

"What's that?" she said. "If it's for the panto, you're too early. Bring it back in December."

Aubrey rang the bell. Dr Dhondy appeared.

"Got a customer for you, Doc," said Aubrey nastily. "See what you can do with that!"

Dr Dhondy raised her eyebrows. She looked at Wagstaffe for some time. She thought. She scratched her head.

Then she said to the nurse in charge: "Have the operating theatre made ready. Call the team. I will start operating in five minutes."

"Yes, Doctor," said the nurse in charge. "Where are you going now?"

"To the garage. There are some things there I might need. Some bits and pieces. And my tool kit."

Aubrey, who was listening round a corner, laughed so hard his teeth ached.

"What a berk that doctor is," he said.

Chapter Fourteen

The Operation

The details of Wagstaffe's operation are so horrible that they cannot possibly be written down. Dr Dhondy worked in a most unusual way.

After the first cut, she pulled out Wagstaffe's heart and threw it in the bin. She tossed away his kidneys and his liver and his lights. Which looked like pancakes, all of them, they were so flat. She pulled out metre after metre of greasy, glossy tubing until the nurses were knee deep.

(Have you ever seen inside a person? We're a pretty gruesome lot, deep down.)

The sister fainted first. The Dr Dhondy's assistant. Then the man on the breathing gear. Then the nurses. Finally, she was all alone. All alone with what was left of poor little Waggie.

"Now," said Dr D. "Let's see what we've got in the bag here."

Wagstaffe – although he would have died if he could have seen himself – was not unhappy about all this, by the way. Because from the moment the lorry wheel had popped him like a bubble of spit, the only thing he'd felt was when the shovel hit him. He lay on the operating table with his eyes open, but he could not see. He could not feel. He could not give a damn.

So Dr Dhondy worked alone. She threw away her scalpel and got a spanner from her tool box. She got a saw, and some clamps, and a sheet of shiny tin. She got some hose pipe, and some small brass cogs, and sixty-seven screws and a yard of baling wire. She pulled a clock to pieces and threw away the hands.

Then she got on the telephone and rang an engineer she knew. They talked for ages.

How was Wagstaffe all this time? Not well, not well.

He had a head, all right, with shoulders and two arms. At the other end his legs stuck out. But in the middle – Oh!

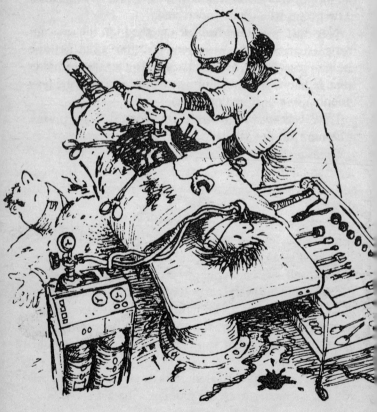

Oooh! Groeugh! When the nurses woke up, one by one, they wanted to faint again. Some of them the doctor sent out, with lists of things to buy on sheets of paper. After six and a quarter hours she had a sandwich.

Dr Dhondy was very popular with the staff. Everybody liked her, almost – everybody except Aubrey and his friends. So when she asked them not to say a word to anyone about this operation, they kept their mouths shut.

"You see," said Dr Dhondy. "What I always wanted to be was a mechanic. If this leaks out, I could be in trouble. The bosses would not understand."

Now that Wagstaffe had been cleaned up, the assistant surgeon and the nurses – everyone – felt great again. Because he looked good now, neat, and tidy and quite smart. Smarter than he'd ever looked before, probably. It's amazing how people like you if you're smart.

"We'll keep your secret, Dr Dhondy," they said. "Doesn't he look smart!"

"He does," said Dr Dhondy. "It's a pity about the key. Smuggle him to a private room until we can see if he's going to work properly. And don't let Aubrey see him."

One of the nurses said: "What about his heart and stuff? People would suspect if they spotted that."

Another nurse said: "I've got a dog. I'll take some of it."

"Pity to waste it on a dog," said another. "He's lovely and young and tender."

They shared it out. They liked a good stew in Oldham.

Chapter Fifteen

Awakening

It was many hours before Wagstaffe came to his senses, and it took him a long time to work out where he was.

First, he did it by smell.

He could smell soap, and medicine, and cloth.

Then he did it by touch.

His face was touching something crisp and cool. His hands were hot, and trapped. His toes would not wiggle.

Then he opened his eyes.

He saw nothing but whiteness. A pillow. His nose was buried in it.

Wagstaffe tried to speak, but made only a muffled grunt. He tried to move, but could only squirm. He was stuck in a bed, face downwards. If he listened hard, he could hear traffic, far away. And a quiet ticking.

A ticking. A gentle, regular ticking.

Wagstaffe went to sleep again. He was very comfortable. Maybe he'd died and gone to heaven. Maybe he was lying on his face in the Great Hospital in the Sky. Maybe they were fitting him with wings.

Come to think of it, thought Wagstaffe, as he drifted off to sleep, I can feel something in the middle of my back. It'll be the wing root.

He moved his head, painfully, and looked out of the corner of his eye. Yes, he could see something. Something flat. Something curved. Something odd.

It was a wing. He'd gone to heaven.

Wagstaffe smiled.

Quite right too, he thought. About time someone realised how good I am.

I've become an angel.

Chapter Sixteen

The Awful Truth

When he discovered just how wrong he'd been, Wagstaffe got very angry, and extremely rude.

Although he hadn't fancied being angel-good, having angels' wings had struck him as very fair news indeed.

But a dirty great metal key sticking out from a polished ring between his shoulder blades was entirely another matter.

"I've never heard anything like it," he stormed at Dr Dhondy. "You're not a surgeon, you're a fruitcake. I only got run down by a truck. Why couldn't I be stitched up like anybody else? Why the key in any case, rabbitbrain?"

"You have a key, Wagstaffe," the doctor replied quietly, "because you have a spring. How else could we wind you up?"

"People *don't* wind up," screeched Wagstaffe. "They don't have springs. They have hearts, and lungs, and stuff like that."

"People," said Dr Dhondy, wagging her finger, "don't have hearts and suchlike if they play sillybees with lorries, do they? Nurse Sadie M'Gee had your heart, with some savoury dumplings and an onion sauce. Very nice it was too, she told me."

Wagstaffe went pale.

"You are joking, aren't you? You haven't really had my heart out?"

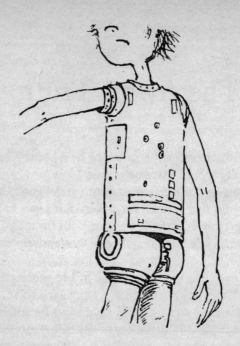

"Heart, liver, kidneys – the lot. By rights, young fellow,
you should be six feet underground. I've saved your life.
And all you can do is cheek me. If you're not careful, I'll
forget to wind you up."

For many minutes, Wagstaffe said not a word. Then he
asked for a big mirror. Dr Dhondy brought one. Wagstaffe
asked to have his clothes off, and Dr Dhondy helped. They
stood side by side, the tall, brown doctor and the white and
skinny little boy. Wagstaffe turned round.

"Oh crikey," he said. "Is it truly me?"

The doctor smiled.

"The key turns this way," she said, showing with her
hands. "That little nipple just above it is the oil point. Two

drops a month, or it might get rusty. Now your front."

The whole of Wagstaffe's stomach was of tin, very shiny. There were metal axle ends here and there, which were slowly twisting.

"These points must be rubbed over with a greasy rag from time to time," said Dr Dhondy. "And you had better keep away from water. Do you wash a lot?"

Wagstaffe shook his head.

"Good. This here –" she poked at a plate below his armpit "– is the emergency panel. There are buttons under it."

Wagstaffe was frightened.

"What emergencies?"

"Oh, if your spring should stick, or a cog should slip, or if you need to have a burst of extra power. Inside here –" Dr Dhondy pointed to the area between his hips "– are some rechargeable batteries. I am making up a lead at this very moment, to plug into the electricity from time to time. Your end will plug into the best place I can think of."

She smiled.

"There," she said. "That's not so bad is it? Better than being dead, in any case. Why do you look so sad?"

Wagstaffe *was* sad.

"I look pretty funny," he said. "It's not very hi-tech, is it? I mean – a *key*. Will I work all right?"

"Oh, I hope so," said Dr Dhondy. "Your joints are very stiff, and you will take some time to get used to yourself. But in many ways, you will be as good as new. Better."

Wagstaffe tried to get his pyjamas back on, but he could not.

"I can't have been very good to start with, then," he said glumly.

Dr Dhondy helped him slowly dress.

Chapter Seventeen

Getting Better

There were some good things about being half clockwork, Wagstaffe discovered over the five weeks that he stayed in hospital. First of all, the eating and drinking.

Being a growing lad, Wagstaffe liked to gobble, but there were not many foods now that did him any good. In fact, the only thing that Dr Dhondy said was exactly right for him was tinned peaches and cream – slippery, full of goodness, and not likely to gum up the works.

But good for him or not, other food could be eaten in any amount he liked. Twenty sausages and a pile of mash, three helpings of apple crumble and ice cream, and a ton of buns. If he felt uncomfortable, he just got rid of them.

This was easy. He opened up the side of his shirt, pulled a clip back, and slid out the metal tray at the bottom of his belly. All the chewed up, churned up, steamy scrag-ends of sausage, potato, custard, crumble and currants could be tossed into the swill bin to be fed to the pigs. Or to the people in the National Health Service Wards. The tray slipped back, and he could start again. A guzzler's dream...

It was the same with drinks. Tea, coffee, lemonade, Coke, anything. He just drank it down until he was uncomfortable, then let it out. Wagstaffe had two cocks for draining, not the normal one. The second was at the end of his right index finger. Dr Dhondy said it would save him a lot of trouble when he was older, and driving along in a car. A lot of time and trouble.

Although he did not mean to, Wagstaffe grew very fond of Dr Dhondy. For starters, she kept him in this private room and brought him everything he wanted, and she listened to him, and she told him jokes, and she taught him how to use his clockwork body, and some of the things it could do.

She also made parts of it better, all the time. She redesigned his oil filters so that they only needed changing once a year, she did his joints out with a new plastic lining so that Wagstaffe could move every finger, toe, leg and arm almost any way he wanted, and she fitted extras like electric lighting in his eyes so that Wagstaffe could see in the dark.

But the key remained a problem. It got in the way, it was almost impossible for Wagstaffe to wind himself, and it looked stupid sticking through his shirt. They often argued about it. Sometimes things got very fierce.

"You stupid, nasty, horrible Toadperson," Wagstaffe screamed one day. "It's all right for you, smug in your white coat. But how am *I* going to walk round in the world with a key in my back? Call yourself a doctor – you couldn't cure the common cold!"

Dr Dhondy was nasty back, and they roared so loudly that patients in other wards banged on the walls with the bits of themselves they could still move. Finally Wagstaffe – very upset – began to cry. Little drops of oil ran down beside his nose.

"I'll never be a normal person again," he sniffed. "I wish you'd let me die."

The doctor patted his head.

"I'll try to improve it, Wagstaffe. I'll try to make it fold away. Oh, if only the hospital had more money. We could use transistors, a microchip, computers. Maybe one day. Maybe."

Wagstaffe still sniffed.

"In the meantime," said Dr Dhondy, "read your papers, and do your exercises."

She paused.

"You're not a normal person, anyway," she said. "You are Wagstaffe, the one and only Wagstaffe.

"Wagstaffe the Wind-up Boy."

Chapter Eighteen

Brandy and Porridge

The papers Dr Dhondy had mentioned were the newspapers. For Wagstaffe, since his accident, had started reading them. All of them, all the time.

He did not read them for the news, though. Or the sport. Or the TV, or the book reviews, or the pictures of the bare ladies in the grubby ones. He read them for the circuses.

Now that was pretty silly. There aren't a lot of stories about circuses in newspapers at the best of times. Only if something really nasty happens, like a big top burning down or a lion eating a nosy boy or something, does it get reported. Circus ladies, although they are often pretty, don't usually have big breasts. So even they don't appear on Page Three.

But almost from the moment he had realised he was alive, Wagstaffe had thought about his mum and dad. He remembered their note quite well: "You will never, *ever*, see us again." He remembered what his dad's headmaster had said: "He's gone to join a circus, I believe." Wagstaffe could only think of one way of ever getting in touch with them again: by reading about circuses.

Why did he *want* to get in touch with them, you may wonder? Well, Wagstaffe wondered it too. They had been horrible to him, they had made his life a misery, they had run away. But now he'd had his accident, he thought they ought to know. He thought they'd be ashamed of

themselves for driving him to it. He thought they'd be full of guilt. He thought they'd grovel and beg him for forgiveness.

He *wanted* to see them grovel.

He *longed* for them to suffer.

And when they'd grovelled and suffered for ages, when they'd cried and screamed and begged and begged and *begged* him for forgiveness... he wouldn't forgive them. He'd tell them to get stuffed.

Wagstaffe could hardly wait.

So every day, he spent hours going through every magazine and paper he could get. He had piles of them all around his bed, and under it, and on the windowsill. He got bad-tempered if Dr Dhondy did not bring at least half a dozen new ones every visit.

It had two very good effects. One, he learned to read very

well, whether he wanted to or not. Two, he became an expert on circuses. He knew every clown by name, the weight of every Fat Lady, the number of nosy lads each lion had had for dinner.

But his mother's or his father's name, he had never seen. Not once. Not even hinted at. When he had told the headmaster he was going to join a circus, his father had been lying, as usual. It made Wagstaffe want to throw up.

"Not fair, not fair, not fair," he stormed to Dr Dhondy one fine day. "Troutfish and the Gribbleworms, that's all they ever write about. Troutfish and the rotten, posey Gribbleworms."

He tossed the *Scum* to the foot of his bed. Dr Dhondy picked it up and looked at the story.

"Circus Stars in New Death-Defying Stunt," she read. "What a headline."

"Well, they do some silly things," said Wagstaffe. "Last week Mr Gribbleworm dived a hundred metres into a tank of hot porridge that Mrs Gribbleworm had poured brandy on to and set alight."

"What a waste of brandy," said Dr Dhondy.

"What a waste of porridge. Still, Troutfish pays, and millions of people come to watch, so I suppose they're all making a fortune."

He sighed.

"And nothing about my mum and dad."

Dr Dhondy stood up from the foot of the bed.

"Never mind, Wagstaffe," she said. "Today I have good news. You are as fit as I can make you. Keep out of the rain and you will be all right. Just one last oil change, and then you're done."

Wagstaffe could hardly believe his ears.

"Done? What do you mean?"

"I mean you can go home. Tomorrow morning. This afternoon the oil, then a check-over, and a good night's sleep."

Wagstaffe gulped. He had to face the world at last.

Alone.

Chapter Nineteen

Going Home

In a naice book, that got awards and was put in the best places in the library by naice ladies who thought it was a naice read for naice boys and girlies, there would be a really soppy bit now.

It would go on for page after page about how the morning dawned bright and clear, with the birds singing, but how Wagstaffe felt somehow sad because he was leaving his friends at the hospital and facing the Great Unknown. It would get pretty damn yukky.

So none of that, eh? Wagstaffe got up, emptied his stomach tray of last night's bread and cheese and pickled onions, got dressed, and got ready to leave. He zipped up his jacket as tight as possible, and called for Dr Dhondy.

"This new key set-up, Doc," he said. "It folds away all right now, but I keep feeling as if it's going to spring out at any minute."

Dr Dhondy felt his back.

"Yes, it is lumpy. But it's the best I can do, Wagstaffe. With luck it'll stay flat. At least you don't need it winding very often now."

That was true. The doctor, egged on by Wagstaffe's moaning, had done wonders with both the key and the main-spring inside him. He was hardly likely to run down when he was not expecting it. But Waggie was an ungrateful little swine.

"If it pops out on the bus and makes me look a fool," he said. "I'll come back and gob in your eye. How often do I need it winding?"

The doctor shrugged.

"I'm not exactly sure. The more you race about, the quicker it runs down. And if you let it go down too far, you won't have the strength to reach behind and do it yourself. You'll have to ask for help. It's all going to be trial and error."

Wagstaffe was furious.

"You're utterly useless, do you know that?"

"And thank you for saving my life, Doctor. And making me work again," said Dr Dhondy. "You really are a rude little slob, aren't you?"

"Knickers," said Wagstaffe. "Give us fifty pee for the bus, will you? I'll come and visit you if I have any trouble."

Two nurses were watching this, quite shocked by Wagstaffe's nastiness.

"Don't mind him," said Dr Dhondy. "He's nervous that's all. He's a little frightened to be leaving here."

Wagstaffe gobbed in her eye.

Chapter Twenty

Eggs and Barking

Wagstaffe Winstanley Watkins Williams was glad to be back to Real Life, once he'd got used to it.

He walked from the hospital rather jerkily, afraid that everyone would laugh at him, and point. But when he spotted himself in a shop window, he was reminded that he didn't look much different from most other boys.

Blue jeans, black windcheater, trainers. The lumps on his back could have been a scrunched-up jersey, and the people on the pavements didn't know what made him tick, did they?

Come to that, he didn't tick very loudly any more. Dr Dhondy had silenced him well.

Wagstaffe waited till his bus came along, paid his money, and hopped upstairs. That was when people *did* begin to stare.

"Oops," said Wagstaffe, picking himself up off the floor at the bottom of the steps again. "I'll take it slower this time."

"Aye," said the driver. "You better had. Is your head all right?"

Wagstaffe rubbed it, pretending it hurt, then began to walk upstairs slowly. This time he did not whizz right off the top step at forty miles an hour. This time he did not hit the metal roof with a dreadful clang. This time he did not bump and bounce all the way to the platform, feeling silly.

Two old ladies on the top deck watched him in amazement.

"Ee, lad," said one. "I wish I could still do that. I were a right goer in my time."

"It's these new breakfast foods they give 'em," said the other. "Look at that dent you've put in th'roof, lad."

Wagstaffe hoped an inspector did not get on. They might make him pay for the damage. He sat still and silent until he reached his stop.

Walking back down the roads leading towards his street was wierd. It was as if he hadn't been back for weeks. He hadn't.

There was a funny smell to the place he didn't remember. A nasty smell. A rotten smell. People were walking about with hankies clutched to their noses.

Wagstaffe saw Hughie N'Dell playing in the gutter with his ferret.

"Hi, Hughie. What's that smell?"

"Hiya, Waggie. I didn't smell anything till you came along. Anyway, I thought you were dead. Maybe that's the pong."

"More like your ferret," said Wagstaffe. "Come on, tell us."

Hughie N just laughed.

"You'll find out soon enough," he said. "I hope you can still run."

Wagstaffe turned the corner into his street. The smell got stronger. It was disgusting.

"It's like the Last Trump," he thought. "What's going on?"

The scene was amazing. Dozens of people in uniform. Dogs barking. Fire engines and police vans. All round Wagstaffe's house.

And everywhere, that smell.

Suddenly, Wagstaffe knew what it was.

"Cripes," he whispered. "I didn't cancel them after the accident. It's eggs. It's rotten eggs."

It was.

Chapter Twenty-One
The Neighbours Complain

Wagstaffe was about to put on a spurt to get to his front door. But when he saw the looks on everybody's faces, he thought better of it. He thought he'd better hide.

He crept along the garden fences until he could sneak behind a house. It was Mr Dickin's, the nastiest of the neighbours. But there was no one at home in any of them. They were in the street, watching.

Along the hedge and behind a clump of bushes Wagstaffe crept. Over the fence he peeped. He pressed a small switch behind his right ear and listened.

He could hear everyone now, even a hundred yards away. At first the babble was horrendous. Then he began to pick things out.

"Seven weeks, two pints a day, a pint of cream, a dozen eggs, a tin of peaches, two yoghurts. I'm owed a fortune."

That was Mr Huddersfield, the milkman. Wagstaffe had not recognised him in his gas mask.

"Never mind the expense! What about the smell? It's disgusting."

That was Lady Potter, the retired gentlewoman who was actually an Oldham slum kid who'd struck it rich.

"Never mind the smell! What about the danger to public health? The rats are so big they've been chasing my dog, Bonzo."

That was Fatty Dickin. Serve him and his soppy pooch

right, thought Wagstaffe.

"It's bringing the house prices down."

"It's getting us in the papers."

"The flies round here are bigger than *Harrier* jump jets."

"And better fighters."

All the neighbours were having a go. Plus a few army officers, policemen, and the local fire chief.

"Who owns it?" said the policeman with the most silver on his cap.

"A most pleasant and respectable couple called Williams," said Lady Potter. "They ran away a couple of months ago."

"To escape from their son, Wagstaffe," added Mr Dickin. "A most horrid child. A disgrace. A horror."

"And where is he?"

The milkman spoke.

"Nobody knows," he said. He sounded rather sad. "I quite liked the lad. He were a bit of a rogue. He promised me he'd pay the bill and I believed him. That's why I went on delivering the stuff."

Everybody looked at the milkman, then at the things he had delivered. There was a pile of egg boxes ten feet high. Milk bottles, some of them smashed by rats, dogs and vandals, littered the lawn. A mountain of rusting peach tins, crushed cartons of reeking, putrid cream.

The police-toff spoke.

"That was a little stupid of you, wasn't it?"

With his special hearing, Wagstaffe thought he could pick up muffled sniffs from underneath the milkman's gas mask.

"I believed in him," said Mr Huddersfield.

Wagstaffe, chuffed by this and annoyed by the way they spoke to the poor old man, jumped over the fence and landed in the middle of the bunch.

"I'm back," he said. "What seems to be the trouble?"

Chapter Twenty-Two
The Big Clean Up

Troubles never come singly, Wagstaffe soon discovered.

All the niceness in Mr Huddersfield disappeared instantly. He pulled out a bill for fifty-seven pounds and handed it across.

"You rat," he said. "I trusted you. If that's not paid by Friday, you'll go to court."

"Prison, I shouldn't wonder," said the police chief. "Have you ever heard of wasting police time? It's very serious, and you've been doing it. I've got twenty men and women on this job."

Several of the neighbours shrieked at him: "You foul little monster. You've ruined this street. We'll never hold our heads up again. It's like the corporation tip. We're suing you for thousands and thousands."

"Talking of the corporation," said a man in a boiler suit and bowler hat. "I'm from the Health Department. It'll take two muckcarts and fifty lads to clean this place up. Two hundred and ninety pounds sixty-four p. By next Monday."

The Fire Brigade wanted a donation, and it turned out the army had sent a helicopter to have a look in case it was a Russian plot. The bill for that was eleven thousand pounds.

Wagstaffe tried to add it up. It came to quite a lot and a little bit more. Roughly.

"I'm going in now," he said. "I've not been well."

The people who wanted money pressed the bills into his hands, and the neighbours, led by Fatty Dickin and Lady Potter, were all for scragging him. The police-toff stopped them.

"Don't waste him," he said. "When he grows up he'll be a real criminal. We'll have him then."

"They may have brought back hanging, with a little luck," smiled Lady Potter.

Wagstaffe went inside for a think. He picked up a couple of tins of peaches on his way. In the upstairs window he ran the tops of the tins off on his special tooth and slurped down the cool, sweet fruit. He sighed.

Outside, the job of cleaning up went on. The dustmen, the police, the lorries, the shovels. The neighbours watched, with looks of disgust pinned firmly to their faces. When Wagstaffe went down to pick up more peaches and a dozen eggs, they booed.

Bored at last with watching them, Wagstaffe went and switched the telly on. As usual, though, the picture was too fuzzy to make out in daylight. Ah well, it would soon be getting dark. It had been a long day.

The eggs in the carton were rotten. Wagstaffe took them upstairs and watched the final moments of the Big Clean Up. The place was empty, almost, the police and dustmen gone. Only a few neighbours hung about.

Far down the street, he could see Lady Potter walking alone, in her fluffy fur coat. The range was about half a mile.

Wagstaffe quickly opened the window and pressed certain places on his head. He began to calculate.

Through the dusk, a minute later, half a dozen eggs flew high into the Oldham air. They went up a long way, and came down almost vertically. One by one, they burst stinkily in Lady Potter's hair. Screaming, she turned to look for Wagstaffe in the street. Of course, he was not there.

A minute later, through the open window of his lounge, Fatty Dickin received the other six. One on his bald head, one in his face, two for the dog, and one each for his wife and daughter Ermintrude.

Wagstaffe was happy. He still couldn't count or do sums. But when it came to ranges and trajectories, or throwing things a half a mile and never missing – well!

It was dark. He thought he'd try the telly again.

Chapter Twenty-Three
Amazing News

On his way to the living room, Wagstaffe tripped over the pile of letters in the hall. He'd seen them earlier, but he hadn't bothered. He'd never read a letter in his life. Or had one, come to that.

But things were different these days. He'd had so much practice in hospital that he could read as well as anyone. Who knew, there might be something from his mum and dad.

Wagstaffe picked up the great armful, and took it to the kitchen table. There were, to his surprise, lots of postcards. Letters in brown envelopes with windows, airmail letters, letters in blue envelopes – and postcards. He picked up the first that came to hand.

On the picture side were two elephants, with hats and earmuffs on, balancing on tubs. Circus elephants. That was peculiar. Wagstaffe turned it over.

"Dear W," it said. *"We are now in Germany. Life is good without you, and we are getting rich. Glad you're not here, Mr and Mrs W."*

Germany, thought Wagstaffe. Gosh, they've got around. He turned over another.

"Life is good in France," the postcard informed him.

"*The circus is at a little town called Paris, which you won't have heard of, being ignorant. We are very popular with the audiences.*"

This card had penguins on the front, one of them playing an accordion. Wagstaffe reached for another.

"*Heard of Prague, Dumbo?*" asked the words. "*That's where we are. We have lots of money and are very happy. What a good idea it was to run away.*"

Wagstaffe was fed up. They must have joined a circus after all. They must be touring Europe. They must be getting on without him. Fine. He tossed the cards away and picked up a letter with his mother's writing on it. Maybe he'd learn more from a letter.

He did. It was two whole pages, and it was sent from Holland, although there was no full address. It had been written five weeks ago.

His mother was bubbling with glee and jollity. She and his father had met a man, she said, a Very Great Man. He had seen their natural brilliance and talent, and trained them up to be an act. He was going to make them superstars.

The next letter Wagstaffe opened – doing it in order, now, by the dates on the envelopes – said that his mum and dad were doing Special Tricks to Fantastic Audiences. The Great Man was a superb teacher – better even than Dad had been.

They could ride one-wheeled bikes, they could be chained in padlocks and tied in sacks and thrown in lakes of freezing water and escape in seconds. They could eat fire, they could chew razor blades, they could walk barefoot through redhot coals.

As a special trick next week, his mother wrote, the Great Man was going to teach his father how to support a railway locomotive on his chest while whistling God Save the Queen. She, Mum, was going to drive a six-inch nail up her left nostril with a gold-plated hammer.

He flipped through the postcards again. From Belgium, France, Denmark, Poland, Luxembourg. From Germany, Ireland, Yugoslavia, Greece. With pictures of lions, tigers, ponies, giraffes and apes. And some people.

Some people. Circus people. Fat men and bearded ladies. Giants and dwarves. Clowns and ringmasters. Acrobats.

And on card after card, a pair called the Gribbleworms. An ordinary enough looking pair, with long blonde hair, both of them, and shiny, sequinned costumes, white and sparkling. The Famous Gribbleworms.

Wagstaffe had heard of them. The ones who did mad stunts. He laughed. Just like his mum and dad said *they* did. Except that no one had ever heard of them!

What's more his mum and dad did not have long blonde hair. His mum's was mousey-coloured and his dad was bald. Typical of them to reckon they could do stunts just when the Gribbleworms were getting incredibly famous, with their superb manager, Mr Troutfish. Typical.

Fed up with letter-reading and looking at cards, fed up with finding no money but plenty of bills among the brown envelopes, Wagstaffe switched on the television. It was the news. It was amazing.

Chapter Twenty-Four
A Spot of Bother

If you watch the news on TV, you'll notice that after all the miserable bits, they have a funny item. This is called Light Relief, and is to stop half the population hanging themselves out of misery. Or worse – switching off their telly sets.

Sometimes it's about a dog that can read and write, sometimes it's about a man who's pushed a stuffed frog three hundred miles with his nose to raise money for charity. Tonight it was about the Famous Gribbleworms.

"The British man and wife who have recently become so famous in the circus world," said the announcer, "are setting off for America tonight to do their most daring trick yet. They will be walking across Niagara Falls on a high wire, with Mrs Gribbleworm balanced on Mr Gribbleworm's head."

A very fuzzy picture came up on the screen. It showed the Niagara Falls, which are big, and very dangerous looking. Wagstaffe adjusted the knobs, but it got no better. The announcer carried on.

"The amazing thing about this latest stunt," he said, "is that Mrs Gribbleworm will not be *standing* on her husband's head, but *standing on her head* on her husband's head. She will also be bouncing a large red plastic ball with her feet. Mr Gribbleworm will be playing a selection of popular tunes on a baritone saxophone."

The next picture flashed up was of the Gribbleworms themselves. Mrs G was holding a beach ball, and Mr G a saxophone. They both looked rather nervous.

"Now," said the announcer. "You must be very pleased and proud about this latest stunt that Mr Troutfish has so kindly set up for you. Can you explain how many years it has taken to train for?"

Before Mr and Mrs Gribbleworm could speak, a large and very ugly man barged into the picture. As far as Wagstaffe could see, he was as wide as he was high. He was as bald as an egg, had wiggly black eyebrows, and smoked a big cigar.

"These two people are wonderful," he said. "They don't need to train. They do it all by nature."

The announcer, who had also appeared, looked puzzled.

"But you must train sometimes?" he asked the Gribbleworms. "I mean, this stunt is dangerous. It's deadly. You'll probably be killed."

Both the Gribbleworms opened their mouths to speak. But the fat man stopped them.

"Remember your contracts, you two," he said. His voice had gone quite nasty. "Let Troutfish do the talking."

"But Mr Troutfish," said the announcer. "I wanted to ask Mr and Mrs –"

Troutfish interrupted him.

"Listen, bum, these two are my property. You speak to me or no one, right?"

The announcer turned to the couple, but Troutfish shouted at them.

"Go! Move! Wait in the car! That's an order!"

As they shuffled off, Wagstaffe knew the truth. He could not see them very well, and he had not heard them speak.

But it was something in the way they held themselves, and moved their legs and arms.

After all, he had lived with them until they'd run away.

Mr and Mrs Gribbleworm, the Famous Gribbleworms, were none other than his mum and dad!

They seemed to be in a spot of bother...

Chapter Twenty-Five

Oil is Thicker
Than Water

Wagstaffe did not even wait to watch Ian McCaskill do the
weather. This was no time for laughter. He went back into
the kitchen, put all the letters and postcards in the correct
date order, and started to read. It was a simple story, and
a sad one.

At first, as well as saying dreadful things about him, his
parents were full of how wonderful they were themselves.
How clever to trick their little boy, and leave him with
nothing, how sure they were that their talent and brilliance
would be spotted.

Then there was a period when they sounded less certain.
Stories of hanging around circuses trying to get jobs. Stories
of cleaning out the elephants' lavatories and polishing the
lions' teeth. Stories of everybody saying they were too old,
and fat, and boring to start being circus stars.

In fact, thought Wagstaffe, they might have been on the
verge of coming back again if something had not happened.
That something was their meeting with The Great Man,
Theocritus Troutfish.

His mother had written:

*"What a wonderful man, you nasty smelly child. If only
you were nice enough to even touch his shoe. He has
promised to make us famous, and extremely rich. He says
there is nothing we cannot do. He has brought us long
blonde wigs and called us Gribbleworm. Isn't that nice*

87

of him?''

There had been a period of terrible, hard gruelling training. Ten-mile runs before breakfast. A thousand press ups. Lifting four hundred kilo weights. Between them, Mr and Mrs Williams had lost ten stones in a week. And got their pictures in the paper six times.

"*Hard work, but so exciting,*" wrote his mum. "*It is a great thing to be famous, awful child. Not that you'll ever know. It is Tuesday as I write this. I wonder if you've cleaned all the nasty brown stains off yet. I doubt it.*"

Then the flying trips to countries near and far. The stunts which got more dangerous, more daring, more exciting. The money going in the bank (so Mr Troutfish promised them).

"*We will be rich,*" one letter said. "*But so far, because of the expense of touring, we have had to help poor Mr Troutfish out. He's taken care of all our savings, the dear man. He says he'll double it when he pays it back. On TOP of our wages! Do you miss us? We don't miss you.*"

The more he read, the more certain Wagstaffe became that his parents were being conned. This Troutfish was a crook, a villain, a rogue. He was making them do things no sane lunatic would do, and taking *their* money as well. He read with horror of the latest plan (three weeks ago) in Hungary.

"*Your dear father is to be fired across the River Danube from Buda to Pest by a giant catapult, wearing only a pair of puce pyjamas and a novelty nightcap. I am to be in a double bed balanced on a fifty-metre pole, pretending to be asleep. Suddenly he will land beside me, to loud applause. Mr Troutfish says we will get a bonus of two thousand pounds for this stunt, but we will have to wait*" *as he is having trouble with the local banks.*"

For the first time, a note of worry had crept in. There was a PS. It said: "*Wagstaffe, this trick is very dangerous. Your father said perhaps we should not do it. It caused an awful row, and we were put into our caravan without supper. I hope he does not miss the bed. Fifty metres is quite a long way to fall on to concrete, isn't it? Is it more or less than inches – I can never remember.*"

They survived the trick, and the next letter or two were jolly again. But very soon Mrs Wilhelmina Williams was sounding terrified. More stunts had been dreamed up, involving cliffs, balloons, gunpowder, dancing on the wings of planes. It also became clear that the caravan was some sort of mobile prison, into which they were locked at night by Mr Troutfish and his enormous minders.

The most terrifying letters were the latest. They spoke of the American tour, with the Niagara Falls high wire trick coming at the end of several days of dangerous and unpleasant routines. Mrs Williams spoke seriously of her doubts of ending up alive.

"*After all, Wagstaffe,*" an air letter said. "*Neither of us have ever balanced on a wire before. And your father cannot even play the saxophone. He's colour-blind.*

Worse, I think that if we get across safely, Mr Troutfish has got another trick or two up his sleeve. Both your father and I wish we were at home. We miss it. We have both been very silly."

Wagstaffe snorted. They missed the house, not him. Well, the whole thing served them right. He turned over the last card, which showed a zebra playing a banjo. Beside the address was written one word: *Help*.

What a pair of pillocks, thought Wagstaffe. He unzipped a tin of peaches with his tooth and sucked the contents down. They were in a mess. They needed help. But they did not even say they missed him.

Did he miss them? Did he hell.

He sighed, and got his sharp tooth in the edge of a second can.

He was their son. He supposed he'd have to see what he could do. He didn't like them much, and they didn't deserve it. But he had a duty.

What was the old saying?

Blood is thicker that water. That was it.

So is oil.

Chapter Twenty-Six
Getting There

Wagstaffe was awoken next morning by a banging on the front door. It was Mr Huddersfield, the milkman.

After a night of bad dreams and worry, Wagstaffe was not going to stand any nonsense.

"I've still got no money, you silly old berk," he said. "Go away before I stick a milk bottle up your nose."

Mr Huddersfield smile. He handed Wagstaffe a pint.

"Get out of bed the wrong side, lad? Here, take your milk. Want anything else today?"

Wagstaffe was surprised. Why the niceness?

"I knew you'd be back in the end," said Mr Huddersfield. "I trust you, Wagstaffe. You're not like your mum and dad."

"Cripes," said Wagstaffe. "Don't you like them either?"

"Like them! They're a pain in the posterior. That's why I carried on delivering every day. I can't wait to see their faces when they come back to that bill."

Wagstaffe looked glum.

"Ah," he said. "Well, that's a problem, see. They may not be coming back."

"Hell fire," said the milkman. "What a laugh! Why don't I come in for a cup of tea?"

"Cup of milk," said Wagstaffe. "They took the kettle with them. And the cups, come to think of it."

Over a tin of peaches and cream each, Wagstaffe told Mr

Huddersfield a little of the story. Not about his clockwork guts, or that his mum and dad were now called Gribbleworm and very famous. Just that they were in trouble in America and needed help.

"I'd let them stew," said the milkman. "Maybe if they die they'll leave you something in their will."

That was a thought. But Wagstaffe remembered Troutfish, and the fact they'd not been paid. No chance.

"I've got to help them," he said. "Whether I want to or not. How do I get to America?"

The milkman scratched his head. He thought for minutes. He ummed and aahed.

"There's only a few things you need to get to America," he said at last. "You need lots of money for your plane fare, you need a passport, and you need a visa. Which one of them three have you got?"

"How much money?"

"Hundreds. A thousand. More. And a visa takes months anyway. You'd probably have to go to London."

"Blimey," muttered Wagstaffe. "In the comics they always stow away. Can't I just do that?"

Mr Huddersfield thought not. Planes weren't like boats, for starters. People had been known to hide in the holes that the wheels went up into, but they were crushed to death on takeoff. Otherwise they froze to death when the plane reached twenty thousand feet. Not much point in that.

"As to ships," he said, "they do still have cargo boats that go there, but they take weeks or months. If your mum and dad need help quickly, they'd be worse than useless."

"Is it far, then, America?" asked Wagstaff. "Where is it, next to Germany?"

Mr Huddersfield shook his head.

"I know school's boring, Waggie, but you are pig-ignorant. It's next to India. Look it up in the atlas."

He finished his milk and got up.

"Forget the whole thing, lad," he said. "I'll let you go on having milk and stuff, don't worry. I'll fiddle it in me books."

Wagstaffe did not reply. He was thinking hard.

Chapter Twenty-Seven
America

Oldham is not far from Manchester, and not far from Manchester is an airport. At 2 o'clock the next morning, Wagstaffe Winstanley Watkins Williams cut through the perimeter wire with his teeth, stunned a guard dog with a blow, and snaked across the tarmac towards the plane he knew was going to America at 7 o'clock. In his back pocket was Hughie N'Dell's passport, which he'd swapped for a packet of Uncle Joe's Mint Balls, and a pound coin he'd stolen from Dr Dhondy's purse.

Dr Dhondy had been very helpful about the temperature at which his body would freeze up, and she'd also told him where America really was, and where to catch a plane. When she'd realised he was serious, she had put a special additive in his oil to make it more efficient in deep cold, and made sure his emergency batteries were well charged.

"The cargo hold of an airliner is very, very cold," she said. "This is all very foolish, you know."

If she thought he was going *inside* the plane, Wagstaffe was not going to put her right. She might try and stop him.

"It's against the law as well," he pointed out. "Don't you mind?"

"Not at all," said Dr Dhondy. "It's much more important to see how your new mechanism behaves under all conditions than to worry about the law."

Which is why Wagstaffe had nicked the quid.

"I don't expect you'll write or anything soppy like that," the doctor told him when he left. "But if you ever return, come and tell me how you got on, OK?"

He nodded. Fair enough.

"And a word of advice, my little wind-up friend," she added. "Don't get wet."

Wagstaffe was surprised at how enormous the wheels of the aeroplane were. Bigger than him. He had to switch his eyes on to full night beam when he was up inside the hole they lived in, to try and find a place where he could perch without getting squashed. I hope *I* don't die, he thought. But he had a nasty feeling he just might.

Unlike other boys, he was able to lock his arms and legs into any position he wanted. So when he'd jammed himself into what looked like the safest place, he could stay there very comfortably. Very soon, in fact, he was asleep. When he awoke, the wheels were up, and he was covered in a thin sheet of ice from head to toe. He couldn't see a thing, and the noise was terrible.

If this is flying, thought Wagstaffe, I don't like it. The view's ridiculous.

His first sight of America – or of anything else – was the tarmac at Kennedy Airport. The ice had melted as they came down, and he was now covered in black greasy smuts from where the tyres had smoked and flamed from hitting the runway. He was hungry.

Did they have tinned peaches in America?

Chapter Twenty-Eight
Cut the Crap

The trouble with writing books – and reading them – is that every now and then you come to a boring part. For example, how did Wagstaffe get out of the airport without a visa? How did he get from Kennedy to New York? What did he do about foreign money? Where, how and what did he get to eat?

You know the sort of thing. In America they call it crap. So let's cut it, shall we? All that's over. He's in the middle of NY, and he's not hungry any more.

But he is lost.

Wagstaffe, as you may have worked out, wasn't very good at geography. Back in England, he had thought America was near Germany. Now he thought that Niagara Falls was probably the same distance from New York as Mumps is from Grotton. He tried to catch a bus.

That part was easy. Although New York is bigger and noisier (and hotter and smellier) even than London (which he'd never been to either) they do have buses. Single deckers, which stop at places marked Bus Stop. Wagstaffe got on the first one along.

"Half to Niagara Falls, please."

The bus driver looked at him.

He was amazed by Wagstaffe's black smutty appearance, and amazed by his accent. He was amazed by what he had asked for.

"Are you a stranger round here, buddy?"

Wagstaffe had seen the Westerns. He knew the language.

"Sure am, buster. Will a oncer do?"

He reached into his back pocket and waved Dr Dhondy's stolen coin. The driver stared at it.

"Are you putting me on, kid?"

Wagstaffe was stumped.

"Putting you on what?" he said, lamely.

The driver put him off. The bus.

It took half an hour for Wagstaffe to find his way to a bus station that did long distance. He learned to his horror that Niagara Falls was hundreds of miles away. Even if his pound had been in dollars, it wouldn't have got him beyond the county border.

He was quite near Grand Central Station. He thought he might sit down and weep...

Chapter Twenty-Nine
Mandy Badsox

Wagstaffe Winstanley Watkins Williams walked towards a public bench feeling bad. He didn't know how to get to Niagara Falls, and he didn't know how to find his parents if he did. Maybe Niagara Falls was a big place too. Maybe they had already moved on, to new and more dangerous pranks.

But as he got close, he saw the advert, huge and gaudy, stuck on a hoarding behind the bench. His heart missed a tick.

It was them. His mum and dad. The Famous Gribbleworms. **HURRY, HURRY, HURRY,** the poster said.

COME TO THE FALLS AND WATCH THE FUN! CAN THIS DARING PAIR DANCE AWAY FROM DEAR OLD DEATH AND PLAY THE SAX AND BOUNCE A BALL! HEAR HALF A MILLION PEOPLE GASP IF THEY WOBBLE! CLAP WITH A MILLION HANDS IF THEY REACH THE OTHER SIDE! GET YOUR *FREE FREE FREE* TROUTFISH MEMORIAL HANKIE TO CRY INTO IF THEY END THEIR DAYS AS MANGLED, BLOODY CORPSES! HURRY, HURRY, HURRY!!

There was a picture of his mum and dad in their blonde wigs. There was a price per person of twenty dollars to watch. There was a date.

Wagstaffe knew the date. He'd seen it in the bus station. He'd missed them by a day. He was too late. They were probably feeding the fishes already. Minced.

Strangely, standing there, Wagstaffe felt he was not alone. He turned his head. A little girl was behind him. She was staring, with a look of complete disgust all over her face.

"Heck," she said. "But you're so *dirty*. People like you just should not be allowed."

Wagstaffe was not in the mood for fighting. He went back to studying the poster.

"Isn't it just marvy?" said the girl, right beside him now. "Me and Mom and Pop are going up to Niagara today to see their latest stunt. They are just so *wonderful,* aren't they?"

Wagstaffe held his breath. This stuck-up little ratbrain was going to *Niagara*?!

"I was just *so* grossed out that we missed the high wire act," she went on. "But Pop was too busy grinding down the poor to go. Parents can be so *gross,* can't they?"

Wagstaffe still said nothing. She eyed him up and down, wrinkling her nose.

"*Your* parents must be *truly* gross to let you walk about like that," she added. "You're filthy. You're horrible. I bet if I called a cop I could have you locked away or something."

Wagstaffe kept his mouth shut. His parents? She'd never believe him...

"Are you dumb or something, kid?" she said. "Has the pussy cat got your tongue?"

She smiled a big smile.

"You're jealous, that's it, isn't it? Because I'm going to Niagara and you're too poor. Hey! I bet you couldn't even afford a burger, could you? And I'm off to the Falls to see the Famous Gribbleworms do their latest trick. Pop says it can't be done. He says they'll be as dead as possums. He says they're crazy."

Wagstaffe could stay silent no longer.

"What is the stunt? Why's it so dangerous? When are they doing it?"

A look of shock came onto the girl's face. She put her nose close to his and squinted at him.

"Where the heck did you learn to talk like that?" she said. "That ain't American. Are you an alien, buddy? Are you

105

from Outer Space?"

Suddenly she smiled, a big, open, friendly smile. She stuck her hand out to be shaken.

"You're cute," she said. "My name's Mandy Badsox. D'you want to come to Niagara Falls?"

Chapter Thirty
Living Rich

It was a long journey, and on it, Wagstaffe talked more than he had ever talked before. He started with his early childhood, went on to his growing up, and continued to the present day. A lot of it was lies, of course. He couldn't let his secret out, under any circumstances.

Wagstaffe talked because Mandy Badsox's mom and pop wanted him to. They thought he was just so *quaint*, and his accent was just so *wonderful*.

When he had said – being very, very polite: "Will you drive me to Niagara Falls, please, sir?" Mandy Badsox's father had replied like this:

"Bo," he said. "Your accent is just too dandy. Keep talking like that, and I'll drive you to the ends of the earth."

When he had met her, Wagstaffe had thought that Mandy Badsox was a pretty foul squitter. Compared with her mom and pop, though, she was terrific. But they were rich, and they were going to Niagara. Wagstaffe could put up with them. Easily.

Mr Badsox was an oil millionaire, or something. He was fatter than he should have been, and he was covered in gold. Rings, wrist chains, studs, you name it. He had a cigar the size of a policeman's truncheon, and a big white hat. He ponged of scent.

Mrs Badsox, however, was worse. Her face looked like a pile of flour with a mouth-shape splashed in blood. She wore a fur coat, a fur hat, and fur earrings. It was summer, and she should have sweated, Wagstaffe supposed. Maybe she did, but her scent made her husband's seem mild.

Although the car was air-conditioned, and quite cool, Wagstaffe felt sick a lot of the time. He was *totally* sick of his own voice. His throat was so dry that he had to keep pressing the small button on the side of his neck for extra squirts of oil.

"Are you all right?" asked Mandy Badsox, when she saw him doing this for the third time. "Is there something the matter with your throat?"

"No, no," croaked Wagstaffe. "It's all this talking. I'm dying of thirst."

Mandy Badsox screeched at her father. "Pop! Stop! This strange boy needs Coke!"

America is big. The roads – freeways – run for hundreds and hundreds of miles. They have petrol – gas – stations, and cafés – diners – and service areas – motels – where you can sleep the night in chalets – cabins. Mr Badsox pulled into a service area.

Mrs Badsox looked Wagstaffe up and down.

"You sure are one dirty child," she said. "You go along to the men's room and wash up. Buy yourself a towel and suchlike from the attendant."

Wagstaffe blushed under the black smuts.

"I'm sorry, missus," he said. "I've only got English money. Will they take it?"

All three of them laughed. Mr Badsox reached into his pocket and pulled out a bundle of notes and some coins. He gave the lot to Wagstaffe.

Ten minutes later, clean and almost fresh, he ate burgers and ice cream, and drank about a gallon of Coke. Followed by some lemonade and a pint of milk.

It was all this that made him give away his secret.

Chapter Thirty-One

Mandy Finds Out

Americans are very well brought up people. In all their mighty land, there's no such thing as a lavatory – they have bathrooms. If a puppy wets the floor, it's called "going to the bathroom on the carpet". If you walk in the Pacific and have a crafty widdle you've "been to the bathroom in the sea". Babies go to the bathroom in their cots.

So when the Badsox family and Wagstaffe were ready to leave the motel, and Mrs Badsox asked him: "Do you want to go to the bathroom, it's a long drive?" you can guess what she meant.

But Wagstaffe, being British, naturally said No. He'd only just had a wash, hadn't he? So here he was, thirty miles down the freeway, dying for the lav.

It wasn't just the Coke and ice cream, lemonade and milk. For Mandy Badsox had been telling him about the stunt they were going to see when they got to Niagara that evening. Which had made Wagstaffe nervous.

"This Troutfish guy, he's wonderful," she said. "He knew a heck of a lot of folk were sick the Gribbleworms crossed the wire without no problems. So he's dreamed up something really smart to follow."

Mrs Badsox said from the front seat: "There weren't exactly *no* problems, honey. Mr Gribbleworm lost his saxophone. And they both hung for half an hour by their fingers."

Wagstaffe's bladder clenched. He'd been shown a picture of the Falls. They were very high and very wide.

"Serves them right," said Mr Badsox. "They shouldn't have tried to change places. It wasn't in the programme."

"Change places?" said Wagstaffe.

"That's right," said Mandy Badsox. "Half way over. Mr Gribbleworm got Mrs Gribbleworm down on the wire and tried to climb on *her* shoulders and do a headstand on her nut. They all but fell."

Mr Badsox laughed.

"That's Troutfish for you, though. Last minute change to please the customers. I never thought they'd live to tell the tale."

Wagstaffe was beginning to feel as if he hadn't been for a week. He crossed his legs. His mum was small compared with his dad. She couldn't have carried that fat swine on her head.

He squeaked: "Do people *want* to see them killed?"

Mandy Badsox looked at him.

"The TV's so goddam boring, isn't it. Hey, Wagstaffe, what's with you, bud? Are you in pain?"

Wagstaffe shook his head. He was going to wet himself.

"What's tonight's trick?"

Mandy Badsox laughed.

"It's terrific," she said. "They're going over the Falls in a barrel. It will be *fantastic*."

Somehow, Wagstaffe was disappointed. He'd expected something worse.

"Oh," he said. "I've heard of that. Lots of people have been over Niagara Falls in a barrel, haven't they?"

"Ah," said Mandy Badsox. "But this isn't a proper barrel. It's made of see-thru plastic. It's lit up from inside.

We'll be able to see the Gribbleworms all the way down. Bouncing and bumping and squawking."

Mrs Badsox said: "It'll be wired for sound. They're wearing padded suits and helmets."

Mr Badsox chuckled: "It's the wildest, fastest, meanest, rockiest river in the world. They'll be like two eggs in a cement mixer. That barrel will reach the bottom full of pink foam."

Wagstaffe could wait no longer. He had wound the window down and put the end of his finger out. He made a noise of relief as all the Coke and milk and stuff squirted into the wind.

It was a bad mistake. Mandy Badsox was staring.

"Wagstaffe," she whispered. "What in heck's name are you *doing*? You're going to the bathroom through your finger!"

Chapter Thirty-Two
Wagstaffe Gets Out!

The sad thing was, that if Wagstaffe had waited for a few more seconds, he could have kept his secret. For Mandy Badsox had hardly had time to start the impossible questions before her father stopped her.

"Quit whispering, you kids," he hollered. "Look over there!"

They looked. On a tall pole beside the road was a big bold notice.

FOLLOW THIS ROAD FOR THE FAMOUS GRIBBLEWORMS. THEIR LATEST – AND PROBABLY THEIR LAST – STUNT STARTS AT 5pm!!!!!!!

"Their last," laughed Mrs Badsox. "I wonder if they'll ever find the pieces."

The next half an hour was frantic. There were signs to be followed, a hotel to be found, a good viewing spot to be paid for.

There was everything to be paid for, in fact, and Wagstaffe was amazed at how much it all cost. Ten dollars here, twenty dollars there, thirty dollars to the man on the corner of the car park. As the whole of America seemed to have turned up to see his parents chopped into little lumps, someone was getting very rich.

115

But however many notes he peeled off from his roll, Mr Badsox kept smiling, and joking, and talking. He booked them into the best hotel on Prospect Point, and gave an extra five hundred dollars to make sure they got the rooms with the best balconies overlooking the Falls. He ordered champagne and lark's tongue sandwiches for after the show, and gave Wagstaffe another big wad of dollars for himself.

"You and Mandy Badsox better amuse yourselves until it starts," he said. "Mandy – here's your cash. We're going to take a shower."

Standing in the foyer of the great hotel, Wagstaffe and Mandy Badsox watched them go. Then she grabbed him by the arm. Hard.

"Right, you," she said. "You've got some explaining to do. Like going to the bathroom out of the auto window back there."

Wagstaffe tried to get away, but she clung on.

"I wasn't, honestly. It's just a trick."

"Huh," went Mandy Badsox. "And what about your back?"

Before he had time to twist, she clapped her hand on his folded key.

"It's all knobbly," she said. "You're wearing a bullet proof vest, aren't you?"

That was good enough for Wagstaffe.

"Yes," he said. "I am. I have to warn you, Miss Badsox, I'm a secret agent. I'm here on a dangerous mission, and there are two armed men on my trail. Oh blimey! There they are."

He pointed to the doorway, and Mandy turned. She was gaping.

Quick as a flash, Wagstaffe jerked free. He ran like crazy to another door. He was gone.

Mandy Badsox stamped her foot so hard it almost went through the hotel floor. She was enraged.

"Wagstaffe," she screeched. "I *hate* you."

Chapter Thirty-Three

The Heavies

Wagstaffe burst into the sunshine certain that she would follow him. Outside, though, he knew he was safe. There were so many people about that an elephant would not have been noticed. Within seconds, the hotel was out of sight. He was invisible.

But Wagstaffe could not relax. There was less than half an hour to go. Among all this jostling throng, in this unknown, crazy place, he had to find his mum and dad.

Where?

First – ask a policeman. A big one was pushing his way through the crowds, sweating.

"Excuse me, sir," said Wagstaffe. "Where do the Gribbleworms start from? I have to talk to them."

The policeman goggled.

"You crazy kid? *Talk* to them? They're famous." His eyes narrowed. "Say, what's with that accent? Are you a communist?"

Wagstaffe ran. Next he asked a shoeshine boy.

"Well, my friend," said the boy (who was about eighty). "I do hear tell the headquarters is over thataway. They got a whole camp load of caravans. I don't know that they'll speak to a little laddie though."

"It's very important," said Wagstaffe. "It's life and death."

The old man grinned.

"Follow your ears then. When the sound of the Falls is loudest, sneak through the fence."

Wagstaffe, hurrying off through all the people, realised for the first time what the roaring noise all round him was. The Falls. Billions of gallons of water hurling themselves to the rocks below. He'd thought it was traffic.

He noticed, too, a great, shiny, shifting cloud low in the sky. That must be spray! Somewhere close to it was where he had to be. He gritted his teeth. There couldn't be much time.

Not long afterwards, Wagstaffe knew he was on the right track. There were policemen about, and PRIVATE signs, and a big wire fence hidden in the bushes. Men with shifty eyes kept peering at him.

Time to go in, he thought. He crashed into a bush like a small tank, and burrowed like a mole. When he came up against thick steel-wire fencing he paused. If he climbed it, he'd go above the tops of the bushes and be seen. This would be a high-energy cutting job.

Wagstaffe Winstanley Watkins Williams remembered Dr Dhondy and all her instructions. He put his hand inside his shirt and pressed buttons. He heard a low humming noise start up inside his body. He seized two strands of the thick, tough, wire and pulled. He pulled and tore, and twisted and bit.

It seemed to take ages, but he was through. In a wasteland of low bushes and stunted trees, with blood dribbling from his fingers and mouth. As he crept along, the noise of the Falls grew louder.

Wagstaffe came upon the caravans too suddenly, and too late. He walked out from behind a bush straight into a clearing. There were men there, with guns and sticks. There were dogs there, with teeth like razors. He froze.

In the few seconds before he was spotted, Wagstaffe saw his parents. They were being herded out from a large grey caravan that had bars at the doors and windows. They were dressed in things like spacesuits, and they had helmets in their hands. They looked utterly unhappy.

In front of them, much as he had been on TV except in ghastly colour, stood Theocritus Troutfish. He was wearing a red jacket, yellow trousers and green shoes. But this time he wore no smile. His face was cruel and taunting.

"Come on, Gribbleworms," he yelled. "Come on, little Englebert and Willie. Your barrel is waiting. It is time to win more fame and fortune!"

He laughed loudly and horribly. In one fat hand he had a whip. He cracked it near their faces. Then he poked Englebert's little pot belly with a revolver.

"There's a million in this stunt, Gribbleworm," he said. "Maybe two if you live. But you'll not see any of it, will you? You know that now, I hope!"

Mr Williams lifted his head to say something, and saw his son. His jaw dropped open.

At the same instant Wagstaffe's mother spotted him. Troutfish followed her gaze. Eleven bodyguards did the same.

The wiggly eyebrows on the ugly face of Troutfish shot

122

to the top of his bald dome and danced a jig.

"Steaming gobsnot!" he roared at his men. "Who's *that* little swine? Where did *he* spring from?"

"Wagstaffe!" screamed his mother. "Run!"

With all the power in his mainspring, Wagstaffe smashed his way into the thickest of the bushes.

The chase was on.

Chapter Thirty-Four
The Chase

The mob of heavies had several advantages over Wagstaffe. There were more of them – about twenty-five in all – they had guns and sticks and dogs, and they knew the area.

On his side, he had surprise, speed – and his secret powers. At the moment, his powers were being used at full stretch.

Wagstaffe thought the sensible thing was to race straight back to the hole he'd already made in the wire. It had cost him a lot of battery and spring energy to do it, and it had taken several minutes. He could not dare to miss it.

He did. Although he reached the fence before even the fastest dog, the hole was nowhere in sight. Wagstaffe cursed, and darted to his left.

Two men were in front of him, with dogs.

He spun away from the fence and crashed back into the bushes. Maybe he could loop round them and find the wire again.

Four seconds and he was in another clearing. A dog sprang straight at Wagstaffe's face, leaving him only just time to raise his fists. The dog's jaw hit them with a trememdous thump. Wagstaffe staggered backwards, and the dog ran off, yelping.

He shot to his right, frantic. But there were men and dogs on all sides. He saw something over his shoulder, turned and lifted his arm to field a heavy stick that had been swung

at him.

The stick snapped, and Wagstaffe's arm did not, although it hurt like hell. But the look of surprise on the face of the thug was good to see.

Ten feet away was the fence. It was appallingly high, with shiny razor wire on the top. But the enemy was moving in. Wagstaffe pushed off another dog, fended another cracking blow, and jumped.

Although he did not clear it, from a standing start he did well. He rose into the air and sailed across the heads of dogs and men. He landed in the wire mesh a metre above their reaching arms.

Then he moved like a rat up a drainpipe, at terrific speed. He balanced on the razor wire, flexed his legs, and sprang. At the last instant he heard a gunshot, and felt a pain in his left arm. He hit the ground – a long long way below – and rolled. A split second later, Wagstaffe was away like a rocket.

The streets were empty now. No cars moved, no people pushed and jostled – even the ancient shoeshine boy was gone. Everyone was in position to watch his mum and dad.

And what could Wagstaffe do to rescue them? Confused and battered, he could not think. For quite a time, he wandered. Precious minutes ticked away.

In the end, covered in grease and blood, he found himself at the hotel. He staggered up the empty staircase, into his room. He had to lie down. He had to rest a moment and to think.

As Wagstaffe threw himself face downwards on his bed, there was a loud TWANG. His key sprang up. It burst through his shirt and jacket and quivered in the middle of his back. The door opened, and Mandy Badsox came into the room.

If she'd been planning to shout at him for disappearing, she changed her plan. She just gaped.

Wagstaffe looked at her, in pain and tiredness.

"Mandy Badsox," he said. "The Gribbleworms are my mum and dad. They've been taken prisoner. I've got to save them."

Mandy Badsox, still astonished, shook her head.

"You're too late, kid," she said. "They've done it. They've gone over the top in their barrel."

Chapter Thirty-Five
The Stunt To End
All Stunts

By a miracle, the Famous Gribbleworms were fished out of the river below the Niagara Falls alive. Their barrel had split and was sinking, and they were bruised and half-conscious.

Wagstaffe watched it on the television in his bedroom with Mandy Badsox, and he could tell they were also weeping, although the announcer said it was just the spray. He noticed something else.

"Look," he told Mandy. "Troutfish is holding a revolver in their backs."

"Baloney," cried the girl. "He's got his arm round them, that's all. He likes them."

Wagstaffe snorted. Funny way he had of showing it! But truly, Troutfish was beaming at the camera.

"I just want to tell the world," he said. "That the Gribbleworms, in my book, are the finest human beings alive today. To endure an ordeal like that and come up smiling is just magnificent." He paused. "To come up at *all* is pretty damn good! And I just want to say, it makes me proud and humble to know them."

At that moment, unfortunately, Mrs Willie Gribbleworm fainted. There, for all to see, was a Smith and Wesson .357 Magnum pointing where her spine had been.

"See!" shouted Wagstaffe. "I told you!"

Mandy Badsox was glued to the set, however. For

Troutfish, rather than being upset, was roaring with laughter.

"Just my little joke," he spluttered. "It's the funster in me I guess. I do so love to interest folks!"

The announcer smiled.

"What a wonderful man he is," he told the camera. "Tune in a little later, when Mrs Gribbleworm has recovered herself, to hear Mr Troutfish announce their next amazing stunt."

Mr Williams, kneeling beside his wife, looked as if he might say something. Then he remembered the revolver. He went on patting his Willie.

"Folks," boomed Troutfish. "Why the hell should we keep you in suspense? Mrs Gribbleworm is a real pro. Even unconscious, she would want the show to go on. I'm going to tell you about it right away."

Mr Englebert Williams stood up. Mr Theocritus Troutfish knocked him playfully down again with the revolver.

"Ho ho," he roared. "My sense of fun. Lie down there with the good lady, Gribbleworm. This is business. This is *my* part of the act."

Wagstaffe's father lay down as asked. There was blood coming from his nose, and his eyes were closed.

"Friends," said Troutfish. "You will not believe this stunt. This is the stunt that will put Niagara Falls on the map. This is the stunt to end all stunts."

Everybody in the TV studio held their breath. The announcer held his breath. Wagstaffe and Mandy Badsox held their breath.

"Mr and Mrs Gribbleworm," said Theocritus Troutfish, "are going over the Falls again. Tomorrow morning, just at noon."

He paused dramatically. He raised his arms above his head, the revolver glinting in the TV lights.

"And this time," he said. "They will be going *without* their barrel."

Wagstaffe breathed out. He sounded very shaky.

"Oh *no*," he said.

Chapter Thirty-Six
Top Security

Like a true showman, Mr Theocritus Troutfish did not announce the full details until a few hours before the show. When Wagstaffe heard them, despite everything, he had to laugh.

He and Mandy Badsox were in his hotel bedroom, where she had been helping him to patch up his damaged parts. She had rewound him fully, clipped the key back into the shaped recess in his back, and stopped the oil leaks caused by the bullet-snick and the bashing.

She had also, because her father was rich and (she told Wagstaffe) secretly terrified of her, managed to get an adapter to recharge his emergency batteries from an American wall socket. She wouldn't plug him in though. She said the place the plug went was "just *too* gross".

"Well," said Wagstaffe. "It was Dr Dhondy's first try at rebuilding a squashed boy. You can hardly blame her. She probably forgot that different countries have different electricity supplies as well. Maybe she could build some adapters in when I get home."

"*If* you get home," laughed Mandy Badsox. But he did not find that funny.

What he did find funny, what made him laugh, was the announcement on the TV news that Mr and Mrs Gribbleworm were making their second trip over the Falls in a pedalo. When they flashed a picture of one up, Mandy Badsox was aghast.

"What are you *laughing* for, you horrible little monster!" she shrieked. "They can't survive on that. They'll be killed in *seconds*. Oh that's *too* appalling!"

Wagstaffe wiped his eyes with a piece of oily rag.

"It's a long story," he said. "It's something that happened to me when I was just a kid. In a way, you see, it serves them right."

Mandy Badsox was upset.

"You mean we're not bothering to save them after all?"

Wagstaffe sighed.

"Oh no," he replied. "We've got to save them all right. Once they go over this time, they're finished. Troutfish must have made his fortune, I suppose. He just doesn't care."

As soon as Wagstaffe was ready to move (Mandy Badsox covered her eyes while he unplugged the electric lead) they raced down into the street to see what they could do. Very quickly, they made a terrible discovery.

There were police, and security guards, and soldiers everywhere. They had walkie-talkie radios, and dogs, and guns and clubs.

What was worse, they had pictures of Wagstaffe, some of which were poster size, stuck on walls and lamp posts. They were, luckily, very blurred and fuzzy, and showed him jumping down from the fence.

Above was printed the word

WANTED

and below

TEN THOUSAND DOLLARS REWARD

Wagstaffe and Mandy Badsox looked at one, horrified.

"It's a good job you're so rich," said Wagstaffe, "or you'd have turned me in."

"Any more cracks like that," she said, "and I damn well will."

Chapter Thirty-Seven
The Tantrum

One hour later, Wagstaffe and Mandy Badsox were back in the bedroom. They were tired, hot and bothered – but they had achieved nothing.

"It's impossible," said Wagstaffe. "We can't even get near the fence. I've never seen so many armed men."

"I've never run so far in my life," said Mandy. "The number of people who thought they recognised you from that rotten photograph! Ridiculous!"

It had been. At least a dozen times the cry had been taken up: "It's him! It's him!" Wagstaffe and Mandy had to run, and twist, and turn and hide.

"Not just me, either," said Wagstaffe. "There were crowds of people chasing lads all over the place. It was bedlam."

That was also true. No boy was safe from mobs of people hunting ten thousand dollars. A fair number of girls had wished they'd had longer hair and didn't wear jeans. Two hundred and eleven males and seventeen females had been taken to police stations.

It had added to the chaos on the streets brought about by the Gribbleworms' latest stunt. News of this had spread by TV and radio all over America and Canada. Even at forty dollars a head no one had been put off. The roads were jammed, the car parks were bursting, the hotels were full.

In the three weeks afterwards, sixty-one pickpockets

claimed they were official millionaires.

Wagstaffe and Mandy Badsox had done everything they knew to get to his parents. But they had been shoved, squashed, squeezed and shaken. Any hopes they had of getting near the river to beg or steal a boat had also been crushed by the hundreds of policemen guarding every road within a mile of it. They were jiggered.

In the hotel room, they could hear the noise outside growing louder all the time. The dull roar of the Falls was lost, as it had been for half the morning. The louder roar was people, thousands upon thousands upon thousands of people.

Who had come to see the Gribbleworms die...

Mandy Badsox put her arm around Wagstaffe's shoulders.

"Do you know, kid," she said. "This room must be the quietest spot there is. Anywhere. For miles around."

Wagstaffe would have agreed with her, but at that moment the door opened. Mr and Mrs Badsox were there, dressed in their garish best. They goggled at the quiet children.

"What in the name of heck are you two *doing*?" screeched Mrs Badsox. "The view out here is just *incredible*! It cost your pa a *fortune!* Come and have a *look!*"

Mr Badsox added: "They're just about ready to start out. You can see the whole goddam shoot. Those poor Gribbleworm jerks are walking to the pedalo."

Wagstaffe Winstanley Watkins Williams went hollow. It was the finish. He had nothing more to say, or do.

But Mandy Badsox did. She pulled her arm from his shoulder, stood up, and faced her parents. She took an enormous breath, and held it. She started turning blue.

"Oh no," wailed Mandy's mother. "Not a tantrum darling! *Please*, diddums! Just tell us what you *want*!"

Wagstaffe watched in amazement as Mandy Badsox built it up. She stamped her feet, she rolled her eyes, she spat with rage.

"Mean! Mean! Mean! Mean! Mean!" she shrieked. "You're so skinny mean, Pa Badsox. You're meaner than worm turds. You're meaner than any man in the world!"

"Honey!" shouted Mr Badsox. "Anything, honey. Just name it and it's yours! I done my best, honey! This hotel's terrific. The view of the stunt is dandy!"

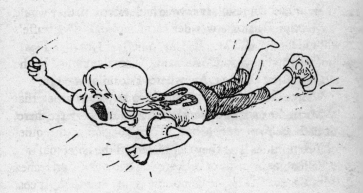

"It's *terrible*," screamed Mandy Badsox. "You'd get a better view with your head in a sock!"

Her voice was becoming so high that it was hurting even Wagstaffe's ears. He pressed a button and muffled some of the sound out. Mrs Badsox had her hands pressed over hers.

"There's only twenty minutes, honey," pleaded Mr Badsox. "It's too late to find another place. I swear to you, the view is wonderful!"

Mandy Badsox threw herself full length on the floor and began to bite the carpet. She kicked at everything within range, knocking over the TV and a tea trolley. She threw a shoe and smashed a picture on the wall.

"The view is zilch! The view is useless! The view is hideous! We need a helicopter, that's what. If you were a proper pa, you'd get a helicopter!"

"But honey," said Pa. "It's too late. Not a helicopter, honey. *How*?"

Wagstaffe realised that Mandy had hardly started yet. She suddenly went bone white, and stopped breathing. She lay there, rigid like a doll. If anyone had walked in, they would have sworn that she was dead.

"Oh God," said Mrs Badsox, quietly. "Not that. Please not that."

Out of the corpse came a voice as cold as the grave.

"Time is running out, Pop. If you love your little girl."

Mr Badsox stared down at his little girl. He stared down at defeat.

Ten minutes later they clambered off the hotel roof into a helicopter.

Chapter Thirty-Eight
Wagstaffe Gets Wet

Wagstaffe had never been in a helicopter before. It was so exciting, he forgot for a while why they were up there.

It was cramped, and noisy, and you could not actually see a lot. You had to crane your neck and peek through thick perspex windows.

Mr and Mrs Badsox had come with them, but they were not happy. Mr Badsox was sulking, and Mrs Badsox was being sick. She was doing it very noisily, and making a vile smell, and dropping paper bags of it out of the helicopter to splat on the heads of the people below.

"We can't keep it with us, can we?" she said, when the pilot told her off. "And they must be poor down there, or they'd be up here. So that's all right."

"Anyway," growled Mr Badsox. "I'm paying for this helicopter, bud. And you. So keep your lousy trap shut."

Mandy whispered to Wagstaffe: "That's money talking, Wagstaffe. Pretty, isn't it?"

Although she'd looked as dead as mutton twelve minutes ago, Mandy Badsox was completely normal now. Wagstaffe asked her how.

"When I lose my rag," he said, "it takes me ages to get right again. It gives me a headache."

"I didn't lose my temper, silly," she replied. "It was one big act. That's how I get my own way. If I have a *real* tantrum I can get anything."

Heck, hought Wagstaffe. A helicopter and pilot was nothing, was it? If he tried that on with *his* parents – his parents! That's why they were up here!

"What can you see?" he hissed. "Have you spotted anything?"

They studied the scene below. The town, looking small and empty from up here. The heads, and hats and sunshades of a million people, colourful in the sun. Ahead of them, the broad river, where it swept towards the Falls.

The Falls. Over to the right of them, stretching for what seemed miles, was the mighty Niagara. Even above the helicopter's engine they could hear its pulsing roar. White water burst over rocks, and from the maelstrom on the other side rose a vast cloud of sparkling spray, which shimmered as it caught the sunshine.

As they moved nearer, the river opened out in front of them, black and empty between the crowds of watchers on the banks. Here and there were rocks, bursting through the rushing surface, blasting foam spouts into the clear, clean air.

Then Wagstaffe spotted it. A small thing on the dark water. An odd thing, painted gaudy red. A pedalo. It was sideways on, being swept ever nearer to the edge.

"Down!" he shrieked. "Down there! Quick, go in closer!"

The helicopter swooped downwards giddily, to the sound of Mrs Badsox throwing up. Soon they could see the pedalo clearly. Wagstaffe could see his mum and dad.

They were wearing ordinary clothes!

His mum in skirt, jumper and headscarf, with dark glasses on her nose. His dad in corduroys and open sandals.

It was horrible! It was Troutfish's idea of a joke!

"They'll be killed," he shouted. "They're only half a mile

away from the edge."

"Less," said Mr Badsox. "Two hundred yards I'd say. Hey, feller, can we follow 'em down in this thing? This is just fantastic!

Mr and Mrs Williams were pedalling as hard as they could, but it was useless. The pedalo was going round in circles. The speed it was approaching the edge of the Falls at was incredible.

"Look," screamed Mandy Badsox. "Helicopters!"

From above them, out of the sun, swept three black 'copters. They were full of police, and bristling with guns. The radio burst into life.

"Get that crate out of here at once," it boomed. "This is private airspace. No one else here by orders of Troutfish!"

"Ignore them!" yelled Mr Badsox to the pilot. "I'm paying for this trip!"

Maybe they heard him on their radios. Maybe Troutfish was just impatient. But the three helicopters opened fire. They saw red flashes from the guns. They heard the bullets screaming through the rotor blades. Mrs Badsox chucked up breakfasts from a week ago.

"I'm getting clear of this!" shouted the pilot. "Hold on tight! We're going home!"

As they pulled round and away from the pedalo, Wagstaffe knew there was only one thing to be done. He thought of Dr Dhondy and what she'd said about getting wet.

He winked at Mandy Badsox and pulled the door open.

"See you, kid," he said.

And he jumped.

Chapter Thirty-Nine
The Brink of Doom

It was a long way down. It was so far down, in fact, that Wagstaffe had time to think, to hear, and to wonder.

He thought it would be a good idea to roll himself tightly into a ball, so that he didn't break an arm or leg off when he hit the water. He did this.

He heard, even above the noise of the Falls and the helicopters, a gasp and then a long, high-pitched Ooooooooooh from the enormous crowd.

He wondered just how serious getting wet would be to a Wind-up Boy, and if he would live to tell the tale. He also wonde—

SPLASH!

He was in. He was cold. He was sinking.

Wagstaffe stopped wondering, uncurled himself, and struggled to the surface. He shook his head, rubbed the water from his eyes, and looked about him.

The pedalo was close. His mother was standing up in it, pointing at his head, and screaming. His father was trying to get her down. The pedalo was rocking madly. Luckily for Wagstaffe, he couldn't see just where the river ended and the Falls began. But the row was deafening.

Even before he had left the helicopter, Wagstaffe had pressed every button that counted. He was on full power, super power. He was immensely strong. He took a breath, got his head down, and swam.

A hundred metres, maybe? Never mind. He did it in eighteen seconds, leaving a wake like a torpedo boat. His mum and dad watched him arrive, shocked into quietness by his speed.

"Hello, Mum and Dad," said Wagstaffe. "I know it's Tuesday, but I thought I'd leave the lavatory. Is that all right?"

They did not laugh. They did not say hello. They sat there, white-faced, as he climbed on board.

"Come on," said Wagstaffe. "Chins up, Mr and Mrs Gribbleworm. Aren't you pleased to see me?"

At last his mother spoke.

"Wagstaffe," she said. "You haven't got the brains you were born with, have you? Why don't you stop talking rubbish and save our lives?"

His father nodded.

"Your mother's right," he said. "If you don't get down

to it immediately, you'll get a smack round the head. Here – have my place."

Wagstaffe found himself smiling. They weren't so bad, after all, were they? Always ready with a merry quip and a kindly word.

"I've a good mind to let you drown," he said.

A terrific lurch as the pedalo hit a rock just below the surface brought Wagstaffe to his senses. He glanced up and almost slipped a cog. They were nearly at the edge. Even he, even on full power – could he?

He jumped into the seat, trying not to look around too closely. He gripped the rudder bar, put his feet on the pedals and began to work his legs.

All around them was a roaring, rushing mass of breaking, churning water. Billions and trillions and zillions of gallons every second were hurling themselves over the huge sheer cliff to the boiling lake below. The river was moving fantastically fast – and faster, faster, faster as it neared the edge.

It all at once occurred to Wagstaffe that he probably couldn't do it. Even a high-speed motor launch probably could not. However hard he pedalled, they'd go slowly backwards until they rested on the lip. Then they'd slide.

Slide and tip. Over and over and over backwards. Hitting the rocks and breaking up. Smashing into chips of bone and gobbets of flesh and brass and tin. He blinked his eyes to clear the spray and sweat. He glanced over his shoulder. There was the lip. Right there behind him. He was right.

They were not going to make it.

Chapter Forty
Things Get Worse

The next few minutes were a blur of noise, effort and agony for Wagstaffe. His legs were going so fast that smoke began to rise from his special knee joints.

"Water," he croaked. "Water."

Mr Englebert Williams, being a teacher, tried to make him drink it, but luckily his mother realised what was needed. She tore off her shoe and scooped water over Wagstaffe's knees and ankles. The smoke turned to steam.

Then his key began to work loose from its clip.

"My jacket," he said. "Get my jacket off."

They tried, they tried very hard. In fact they almost had the pedalo over at one point. But getting a coat off someone who is pedalling a pedalo at twenty miles an hour is not easy.

Then – when the pain was becoming awful – the seam down the back split. The key burst out and stood in Wagstaffe's back, silver and odd.

"What's that!" yelped his mother. "Oh Wagstaffe, you naughty boy! What have you done to your jacket!"

It was impossible for Wagstaffe, even going flat out and then some more, to move the pedalo directly against the stream. But after a few minutes of keeping it hovering six feet from the brink, he found that he could move it sideways.

He pulled the rudders gently to the left, while putting on a spurt. The pedalo slid across the water, rather like a crab. Slowly, crabbily, he started to move it to the shore.

Then they heard the new noise. Over the impossible roaring of the Falls they heard a booming sound, deep and low. Even in the depths of his pain, Wagstaffe wondered what it was.

But his parents knew. They'd heard it before. To them, it was the worst sound in the world.

"They're booing," said his father. "Oh Willie, what a thing to happen. They're booing the Famous Gribbleworms."

"Don't think I'm ungrateful," said his mother to the steaming Wagstaffe. "But this is all your fault."

Wagstaffe, good son that he was, did not stop pedalling and let them drown. But he was tempted. He was sorely tempted.

They were a prize pair of parents, and no mistake. They were the pits.

Not only that, they were stupid. For as the pedalo edged slowly, very slowly into the shore, a new danger appeared. An even worse danger than the Falls, maybe.

But Wagstaffe's mum and dad did not even realise it...

Chapter Forty-One
The Badsox Brigade

The sight of the fat and evil Troutfish, looming out of the spray as they neared the land, filled Wagstaffe with horror.

He was surrounded by armed men, and there were three helicopters parked behind them.

Behind *them* were the baying millions, determined to tear down the wire fence and get their money back.

What did the Gribbleworms say?

"Oh!" said Mrs Gribbleworm. "Isn't that nice? Mr Troutfish has come to meet us!"

"Huh," said Mr Gribbleworm. "He's gone too far this time. I'm going to give him a good telling off."

Wagstaffe, too tired to go back, could only go on. When he felt the floats of the pedalo touch the shingle beach, he almost passed out from exhaustion.

"Hello!" called his mother, gaily. "We're back!"

Snarling, Troutfish's armed guard jumped forward. They dragged the Famous Gribbleworms out by their hair and turned their guns on them. Even the huge crowd fell silent.

Theocritus Troutfish walked down to the water. He stared at the key in Wagstaffe's back. He stared at the small boy who had driven a pedalo against the power of a million engines.

"I like you, boy," he said. "I don't know what your secret is, but I aim to have you in my circus. You and me are going to make a billion dollars."

The Gribbleworms, who by now had got the message, both shouted at once.

"You can't do that! You haven't paid *us* yet! We've got a contract!"

Mrs Gribbleworm added sulkily: "In any case, he's our son. He doesn't even wash himself properly."

Mr Troutfish had a grin all across his ugly face.

"Your son, eh? Well, that makes it that much easier, doesn't it? He can use your contract. Boy – you now belong to me."

Mrs Gribbleworm stamped her foot.

"We'll only let you have him if you increase our wages," she said. "That's fair, isn't it?"

Troutfish laughed. He spoke to his guards.

"Put them back in the pedalo and shove them off," he said. "They haven't finished their stunt."

The pandemonium was terrific. The crowds were cheering again, Mr and Mrs Gribbleworm were swearing, screaming, shouting. Poor Wagstaffe was making a little mewing, helpless noise, like a kitten. He was knackered. Absolutely one hundred per cent.

As the bullyboys pulled him out of the pedalo and shoved the Gribbleworms back in, a helicopter swooped out of the mist cloud and landed on the beach. The door burst open and Mandy Badsox appeared, with a sub-machine gun.

"Wagstaffe," she yelled. "How about this eh, kid? It's the Badsox Brigade!"

Then she snarled: "Drop your weapons, punks, or you're all dead men."

Troutfish was furious.

"Stand firm, men," he shouted. "Fight back. Cut the little vixen down."

The armed men looked the little vixen over. The little vixen smiled. They dropped their guns...

While she covered everyone, Mr Badsox hustled the Gribbleworms into the rescue 'copter. He carried Wagstaffe, who could not walk.

"You'll pay for this," screamed Troutfish. He was black with rage. He was dancing up and down. "These people have spent good money to watch some sucker die!"

The crowd took up the theme.

"Spoilsports! Spoilsports! Spoilsports!" they chanted. "What about the stunt?"

Mandy Badsox laughed. She walked to Troutfish and poked his gut with her sub-machine gun.

"Go on then, Fatso," she said. "Shift your big blubbery butt into that pedal-boat. Give the folks a laugh."

"What! Me! The great Theocritus Troutfish!"

The crowd went bananas.

"Troutfish!" they chanted. "Troutfish! Troutfish! Troutfish!"

He fell on his knees, he slobbered, he wept. But Mandy Badsox had no mercy.

"I'll give you three," she said. "One... two..."

She showed Troutfish the knuckle of her trigger finger. It was white. He got into the pedalo.

"Enjoy your trip," she said. She pushed the pedalo off with her foot. Frantically, Troutfish scrambled for the seat.

"I'm not strong enough!" he wailed. "I'm just not strong enough!"

"Just think of the money you're making," said Mandy Badsox. "And do your best!"

Chapter Forty-Two
Flight

Although Mandy Badsox kept the heavies covered from the doorway as her helicopter lifted Wagstaffe and the Gribbleworms away from the Falls, the men were not interested in trying to shoot them down.

As soon as Mandy was out of range, they grabbed their own guns and raced for their helicopters. But they did not give chase. They were trying to save their master.

Poor old Troutfish was a sad sight. His pedalo was perched on the lip, surrounded by spray from his spinning paddles. It was very colourful – red, yellow, black and green. Like a jellyfish being attacked by a shark.

The Badsox helicopter disappeared into the mist cloud before they saw what exactly happened, but the pedalo floats had cocked upwards and pointed to the sky, so Troutfish was finished. His 'copters would follow the piteous cries all the way down the Falls and try to pick up the little pieces.

Up in the air, Mandy Badsox was winding Wagstaffe up, while his parents told her parents how wonderful they (the Gribbleworms) were.

"Such a pity that he spoiled the stunt," Mrs Gribbleworm cooed. "But then, he always was quite useless."

Mandy Badsox said: "You are now, Waggie. You're coming out in rust, did you know that? And you're all squeaky and stiff."

"I can feel it," whispered Wagstaffe. "Still, at least I'm alive. Thanks."

"Think nothing of it, kid. Hey, I did all right with a plastic gun though, didn't I?"

Wagstaffe goggled.

"Yeah. Pop drew the line at a real one. I could hardly complain. It was hard enough getting him to bribe the pilot to do the rescue."

"I can imagine," said Wagstaffe. "How did you do it?"

Mandy Badsox giggled.

"Another tantrum," she said. "A humdinger. A dilly.

You ought to learn the trick, Wagstaffe. Very useful."

"You must be joking. My parents wouldn't even notice..."

The helicopter took them to the airport, and Mr and Mrs Badsox's private jet flew over from Texas to pick them up. It was only a couple of thousand miles or so. For a week, Wagstaffe lazed about.

The house, of course, had everything. Tennis courts, pool rooms, jacuzzis, swimming baths, the lot. But Wagstaffe stayed indoors, with Mandy Badsox. She was trying to save his life again.

It was a losing battle, though. Between them they used three litres of oil, and a lot of fine sandpaper. But the rust was spreading, all over his chest and back and joints like some funny-coloured rash. Wagstaffe was getting ever stiffer, and more bent.

One day he said to her: "I've got to go, Badsox. I've got to get back to Britain and see Dr Dhondy. I can't even tie my shoelaces any more."

Mandy Badsox knew he was right.

"But can you afford the treatment?" she asked.

Wagstaffe grinned.

"It's free," he said. "In any case, I've got a quid. She'll be glad to see that back!"

Mr and Mrs Williams (or Gribbleworm, as they *still* liked to be called) did not want to leave America.

"We haven't had our pay," they grumbled. "Troutfish must be sued. Anyway, this house is nicer than ours. And you probably *never* cleaned the lavatory when we'd left."

"You can't sue a corpse," said Wagstaffe. He thought of all the unpaid bills at home. That was funny. He did not tell them *they* would be sued when they returned to

Oldham.

There was another reason to leave. Mandy Badsox had whispered it to him in bed the night before.

"Waggie," she said. "Don't trust my Pop. He likes to earn a buck any way he can. I keep finding him reading circus magazines and looking at your key."

"Bloody hellfire," said Wagstaffe (getting in practice for Oldham swearing). "Can't you trust anyone these days?"

"You can trust me," said Mandy Badsox. "And Dr Dhondy sounds all right. But apart from that..."

So one day, they were gone. Soaring across the Atlantic using money his parents had borrowed from the Badsoxes, and the passport Wagstaffe had swapped from Hughie N. Almost the whole flight was an argument.

"It was all your fault really, Wagstaffe. You must admit it," said his father. "Mr Troutfish would have paid us in the end."

"I know!" said his mother. "Let's take it out of his pocket money! How much are we owed?"

Mr Englebert Simpkins Watkins Williams Gribbleworm pulled a grubby piece of paper from his pocket.

"Two million seven hundred and twenty-three dollars, forty-seven cents," he said.

"Right," said Mrs Wilhelmina Winstanley Watkins Williams Gribbleworm. "We'll start next week, you nasty, greedy boy."

The intercom announced that the plane was approaching Manchester airport, and they should fasten their belts.

"And another thing," said his mother. "Keep that lump on your back well hidden when we go through Customs. It's disgusting. And stop that silly squeaking noise."

"And *please* drop that stupid, childish limp," his father

added. "You're a big boy now."

Wagstaffe Winstanley Watkins Williams looked at the airport below, and dreamed about boiling them alive in sulphuric acid. Or was that too good for them?

He'd see Dr Dhondy soon. She'd come up with something.

And he'd have a nice big tin of peaches. With a great deal of double cream.

The Third Class Genie

Robert Leeson

Disasters were leading two nil on Alec's disaster-triumph scorecard, when he slipped into the vacant factory lot, locally known as the Tank. Ginger Wallace was hot on his heels, ready to destroy him, and Alec had escaped just in the nick of time. There were disasters awaiting him at home too, when he discovered that he would have to move out of his room and into the boxroom. And, of course, there was school . . .

But Alec's luck changed when he found a beer can that was still sealed, but obviously empty. Stranger still, when he held it up to his ear, he could hear a faint snoring . . . When Alec finally opened the mysterious can, something happened that gave triumphs a roaring and most unexpected lead.

A hilarious story for readers of ten upwards.

The New Noah

Gerald Durrell

Boa-constrictors, paradoxical frogs, hoatzins, bush babies and tucotucos – they're all part of what Gerald Durrell casually calls his 'big family'. Each animal in his menagerie exhibits such curious habits and eccentricities. There was Cholmondely the chimpanzee, for example, who was 'king' of the collection, liked a good cigarette and his tea not too hot, but had a horror of snakes! Cuthbert the curassow loved to collapse across people's feet when they weren't looking.

Gerald Durrell describes not only the capture of these rare and exotic animals in Africa and South America, but also the problems of caging and feeding them. Footle, the moustached monkey, insisted on nose-diving into his milk, while the Kusimanses – nicknamed the Bandits – found Durrell's toes the most delectable thing in camp!

The Donkey Rustlers is also in Lions.

Ghostly Companions

edited by Vivien Alcock

A brilliant collection of ghost stories written with superb skill in the blending of the natural and the supernatural. Settings vary from the familiar local common and the dusty office to the exotic atmosphere of Venice. The typewriter keyboard with a life of its own, a figurehead that is more than it seems and many more unusual happenings make this collection a feast to satisfy all tastes.

Beyond the Dragon Prow

Robert Leeson

The prophecy at Stiglaf's birth, the crippled son of a Viking war lord, of never ruling his people seems to be coming true. When his father dies, he is challenged to the leadership by his cousin Torald, and forced to flee the land. His wanderings lead him into many exciting adventures with his unusual companions and Stiglaf proves to have other strengths, which enable him to fulfil the prophecy in a strange and positive way.

"A good story, exciting, fast moving, easy to read."
Children's Book Review

Alan Garner

The Weirdstone of Brisingamen
The Moon of Gomrath
Elidor

When Alan Garner's first book, *The Weirdstone of Brisingamen*, was published he was hailed by reviewers as a great new writer. *The Weirdstone* and its sequel *The Moon of Gomrath* are fantasies of striking imagination and power set around Alderley Edge in Cheshire where Alan Garner lives.

Alan Garner has been described in *The Times Educational Supplement* as "one of the most exciting writers for young people today. He is producing work with strong plot structure, perceptive characterisation and vivid language. Furthermore, there is in his writing a basic integrity within which the poetic imagination may have free rein. It is a combination of qualities that creates literature that will be read and read again."

My Mate Shofiq

Jan Needle

Since his best friend got himself killed playing chicken on the railway line, Benard Kershaw has been at a loose end. He's got a gang, including a dead smart girl called Maureen, but they don't do the sort of exciting things they used to.

His life at home's a mess as well, because his mum is ill in a way he doesn't like to think about. Although he still dreams about being a secret agent, or winning the war single-handed, things aren't really all that good.

Then one morning he sees the quiet Pakistani boy in his class turn into a violent fury to sort out a gang who are stoning some little "curry kids". Bernard gets involved, without meaning to at all, and finds himself up against the toughest bullies in the school.

He also finds himself in trouble of a different kind. For Shofiq's family, too, are in a bad way, and the grown-up people who are trying to help them appear to the boys to be set on breaking up everything.

Their attempts to stave off these disasters, and to make some sense of the things they see happening all round them lead Bernard and Shofiq into confusion and violence.

"It's an angry and powerful novel – but much of it is very funny. The characterization is excellent; the dialogue is vivid. Thoroughly recommended."
Reviewsheet

Daredevils or Scaredycats

Chris Powling

"Thanks for saving my place, Mush. I'll have it now."

Fatty Rosewell was a big bully. Every Saturday he used threats and fists to get himself one of the best places in the cinema queue. When Fatty picked on David Clifford, he was looking his most weed-like, all glasses and hair, but weedy David gave all the kids in the queue, not least Fatty Rosewell, a big surprise that morning.

Sometimes it's hard to know where cowardice ends and bravery begins. The most unlikely scaredycats can suddenly turn into heroes. In the course of their adventures, Teddy, Kit, Pete and Jimmy begin to find out just how many different kinds of courage there are.

"Entertaining and realistic, the stories take us into a world of dare and counter-dare, bluff and counter-bluff, catcall and playground scuffle."
Recent Children's Fiction

'Maroon Boy

Robert Leeson

When Matthew Morten went to sea in 1568, he was a Bible-reading merchant's apprentice and the youngest hand aboard *The Golden Way*. He returned four years later with a reputation that included mutiny, raiding, and the nickname ''Maroon Boy'.

'Maroon is short for Cimaroon, a name given to escaped slaves who fought the Spanish in Panama and the English in Jamaica. It is known that Drake joined forces with the Cimaroons at one time, to harass the Spaniards: but where he was seeking gold, the Cimaroons wanted revenge on the white man.

Matthew Morten's motivations were even more complicated – though he didn't realise consciously what they were. Why he did what he did adds a fascinating moral dimension to this tale of swashbuckling adventure.

The Silver Crown

Robert O'Brien

"She did not know how late it was, nor how long she had been asleep, when she was awakened by a loud squealing of brakes, a long and frightening screech of tyres. The car stopped so abruptly that she was thrown forward and hit her head on the button that snaps the glove compartment shut . . . Ellen saw lying inside a pistol with a long barrel she recognized instantly, and a shimmering green hood with two eyeholes staring vacantly up at her."

Fear gripped Ellen. Who was this Mr Gates? Why had he been so keen to give her a lift? And was that the green hood the robber had worn? This was only the start of her long journey, in which the silver crown played a mysterious part.

"No doubt about the impact of this strange, eerie, absorbing book."
Naomi Lewis